As Good as Dead:

The Penelope Stout Story

By Paula E. Phillips

PublishAmerica
Baltimore

© 2004 by Paula E. Phillips.
All rights reserved. No part of this book may be reproduced, stored in a retrieval system or transmitted in any form or by any means without the prior written permission of the publishers, except by a reviewer who may quote brief passages in a review to be printed in a newspaper, magazine or journal.

First printing

At the specific preference of the author, PublishAmerica allowed this work to remain exactly as the author intended, verbatim, without editorial input.

ISBN: 1-4241-0903-5
PUBLISHED BY PUBLISHAMERICA, LLLP
www.publishamerica.com
Baltimore

Printed in the United States of America

*For Jamie, BreAnna, James, Mom, Dad, Benny,
Sarah, Trey, A.D. and Mary Phillips, Aunt Redi,
MawMaw and Buck and all of my family.
Thanks, also to Karen Yerbey for
making me finish what I started.
Thanks to Judith Black, Barbara Harrison,
the Jacksons—Aubrie & Bessie,
Robert Bullard, Ernest Campbell, and
all the other teachers who encouraged me
to write and try hard at everything I do.*

Penelope Stout

"The origin of this Baptist family is no less remarkable: for they all sprang from one woman, and she as good as dead..."

Benedict's History of the Baptists 1790

Chapter 1

The Long Voyage
Summer 1642

Penelope sighed as she looked over the edge of the boat, her prison for almost eight weeks. She could see the vast endlessness of the Atlantic Ocean and how it met the afternoon sky at the horizon with total indifference. She almost smiled sarcastically when she was hit with the notion that this Dutch boat, the *Kath*, and she were so much alike. *How odd we are,* she thought.

The *Kath* was at the mercy of outside forces: the ocean, the wind, and the weather. The sea dominated the vessel in almost every aspect. Yes, the sea allowed the crew to plot the course and steer, but ultimately it was only a man-made plan, feeble at best. The ancient sea would determine the true course. The sea knew this and appeared to hold its secret from the boat and crew. It laughed at the ignorance of man. The sea had its own ideas.

Penelope realized how she, too, was at the mercy of outside forces, first by her religious, strict, and overbearing father, and now by her young husband. She had no course independent of other

CHAPTER 1

factors. Like the little vessel, she could steer no course on her own, take no independent action, nor have any adventures outside of the forces that dictated to her.

Her thoughts turned to her new husband, stuck in the cabin with fever. He was finally resting after two nights of fitful sleep. The fever he had caught after only a few days at sea caused him to come and go out of consciousness. He had steadily gotten worse over the last couple of weeks.

She felt pity and obligation for her twenty-one-year-old groom. She had always had the trait of loyalty. It had not been learned, but something she had been born with. She imagined that she had inherited it from her mother, the woman who had given her life, whom she did not know. Something down inside of her would not let her leave him for very long at a time. It was not love that made her tend to his needs, but loyalty, her birthmark.

She remembered the day she found out she was to marry Kent Van Princes. She had turned nineteen the day before. Her father informed her over dinner of the arrangement he had made with a baron for her hand in marriage. He said that she was old enough to understand and should just accept the blessings he had bestowed upon her. He had found a good man of good faith and well propertied. Any woman would be happy with this arrangement.

Penelope had known that something was being planned. Her father had been writing more than usual lately. He called it some kind of treatise, religious rhetoric she guessed, for it had been religion that had brought him to the Netherlands. He did not believe in infant baptism and had said so. He believed in the priesthood of the believer. He had voiced his opinion on that in England, too. This, of course, had made both the Catholics and the Church of England angry with him. They had called him and others like him "Anabaptists." Those who said it meant it as an insult, but those who received the name learned to wear it as a badge of honor. His only recourse, other than torture and death, had been to escape his native land, so he had brought his pregnant wife to the Netherlands, where Penelope had been born.

AS GOOD AS DEAD

It was this new country that had rescued Reverend Thomson, but at a price. His beautiful, loyal, and adored young wife of three years died giving birth to their only daughter. Two lives were spared at the price of one. It was not fair, but it was how it was. The experience had left the minister with little tolerance for those who did not share his passionate views of religion, for his beliefs had cost so much.

Looking back, the reverend had been mentioning more often that a woman her age should be married. Penelope had not paid much attention at the time. She did not want to be married with the responsibility of someone else to care for. As an only child of a demanding father, she had enough of responsibility. She wanted to be a free spirit, to experience life outside a "woman's" place. She yearned to laugh and to love and to run. These dreams of hers did not include those outside forces her father had designed for her.

Kent Van Princes had been something of a surprise to Penelope Thomson. She had made up her mind not to like him at all, but like a good daughter and servant, to endure the torture of a loveless marriage. Much to her amazement though, her father had chosen not an old and ugly man with smelly breath and cold hands, but a young, articulate, and considerate man. Upon meeting Penelope, he had complimented her blonde curly hair and how he liked the fact that she was not as tall as he. He told her he liked her silky voice. She enjoyed listening to him speak. He spoke of art and literature, all of which intrigued her. He was intelligent and somewhat handsome, well groomed anyway. She found that she did not love him yet, but liked him considerably well and that was more than she had expected.

In return for Penelope's hand, the baron had arranged for Reverend Thomson to have his religious treatise published. Kent had also arranged for the newlyweds to spend their honeymoon aboard a West India Company ship to the New World. All these arrangements had been made in advance and without Penelope's consent. She might have wanted to go and would have been delighted to have had her opinion asked. It was, however, a man's world and it did not matter what she wanted. Kent sought financial opportunity and Reverend Thomson sought religious opportunity. Penelope had to

CHAPTER 1

just go along for the ride and for whatever opportunity happened her way.

Suddenly, her thoughts were interrupted by something that sounded like words. She turned. It was Dirk Bakker, the boatswain.

"Excuse me, Baroness Van Princes. Are you all right? You are not ill, too, are you?"

Startled into this world by the words, she smiled. "Oh, Dirk. It's you. I'm sorry; I didn't hear you until now."

"No matter, ma'am." Dirk was a kind little man with blonde hair and reddened skin from too much sun and salt water. "I was just going to the galley for a bite. Would you care for something, too? You need to keep your strength up."

Penelope looked at Dirk with friendship. She thought about how kind his eyes were. "No. Thank you, Dirk. I'm not hungry. You go on."

"Yes ma'am. The baron, how is he today? Is he better?"

"I am afraid not. He is sleeping now so I took the opportunity to step outside for some air. Mrs. Zant is in the cabin now and said she would stay until I returned."

The twenty-three year old sailor looked up at the sky that Penelope had just been admiring. He looked through the eyes of an experienced sailor, though, instead of the eyes of a dreamer. Penelope wondered at the idea that this man, only a few years older than she, had seen more of the world in one year than she had seen in a lifetime.

"Looks like we may get a storm by morning. You should not be up here much longer. The storms at sea can get very ugly. You don't want to be on deck when the waves peak." His weathered young face had become serious.

"Thank you. I am just going back now."

"Yes ma'am." He turned and went on about his business.

She watched as her new friend went on his way to the kitchen, or galley, as the nautical people called it. She knew she had probably been away from Kent long enough anyway. Gathering her dress, she started on her way back to the cabin they shared with six other people.

Penelope opened the door and looked at her new husband on the tiny makeshift bed. Sweat beaded on his pale forehead. His blonde hair was wet and stuck to the side of his face. The ship rocked back and forth like a cradle for her sleeping husband. His perspiration had soaked the sheet he lay on. He had caught a fever only two weeks into their journey. His medium build frame seemed even smaller to her now and his uncalloused hands were limp, his body lifeless. She clung to hope that this sickness would pass if not on ship, as soon as they got to New Amsterdam where a doctor would be found for him.

"He has not stirred since you left. I opened the porthole in here to let some air in. I thought it might do some good for him to have some fresh air," Mrs. Zant said.

Penelope looked at her older cabin mate. Mrs. Zant was kind and motherly. Her flaming red hair was beginning to grey and her eyes showed the signs of years of smiling. She was in stark contrast to her tall, balding husband who looked as if his face had not seen a smile in a decade.

She was thankful for the help. Beatrix Zant had been the only one of the passengers to offer to assist the young couple. Most passengers avoided the woman with the sickly husband for fear of contracting a disease. Being an older woman of forty, Mrs. Zant understood how overwhelming it could be for a young bride in a difficult situation.

"Thank you. I am sure it helps him," Penelope said. "The boatswain said that we may have some bad weather later on tonight so it will be good to have fresh air while we can keep it open."

Mrs. Zant smiled at the young woman. The smile was warm and tender. Penelope imagined that her own mother had been somewhat like Mrs. Zant; at least she hoped she had been.

"I think I will take a little walk on deck before the weather gets bad then. I will see if I can find Mr. Zant."

She opened the tiny cabin door and disappeared. Penelope turned back to Kent. She wanted to think about their future. Right now Kent's did not look very bright, but she would not give in to that thought. She imagined a fine house in New Amsterdam. After all, her

CHAPTER 1

father had said it was just like old Amsterdam. She would have flowers, a vegetable garden, and many children.

She and Kent had only once consummated their marriage. They had spent their wedding night in an inn close to the harbor. That was the night before they were to set sail. Kent had said they were supposed to have had a private cabin on this little vessel, but there was some sort of mix up in the arrangements. They ended up in this small community bedroom with six other people. It was not at all conducive to romance. Then Kent got sick and, even if they had had some privacy, he could not.

There was a knock at the door. Mrs. Zant's two teenaged daughters, Anke and Neve, came in. The blonde haired young women were fifteen and thirteen, respectively. Each was tall and with flawless skin. Their dresses hid their long legs. Penelope admired their beauty and the glow of innocence that only the carefree young have.

Not wanting to get too close to the invalid on the bed, they stepped as far as they could around Penelope to the low hammock they shared. They sat down and immediately started chatting as young girls do.

Penelope looked at them and it reminded her of the fact that it had only been days ago when she was like that…carefree. She felt as though it had been a lifetime ago. Life for her now was slow and burdensome. It made her feel better to hear such girlish talk again.

The air from the porthole was beginning to get cooler and it felt like the boat was rocking more fiercely. It was not a violent rock, but just somewhat more pronounced. Kent groaned at the movement.

"Did you hear about the savages in the New World?" asked Neve in a loud whisper.

"Yes. I heard the crew talking about them yesterday. The savages hate anyone with blonde hair and blue eyes," Anke replied.

Both girls had golden locks of hair braided and tied with pretty blue bows. It was their only vain decoration. Their parents, like Penelope's, were very religious and would not let their children wear vanity trinkets, but the girls, teenagers as they were, persuaded their parents into letting them have ribbons in their hair. It was out of "necessity" claimed the girls. They had to keep their hair bound. They just happened to have blue fabric that would make pretty bows. They played with their braids as they spoke to each other.

Penelope's ears perked up at the girls' gossip. She had heard tales of murder and violent attacks on Dutch settlers. They were only fairy tales designed for faint-hearted people. Nothing like that really happened.

"I heard that they destroy anything they come in contact with," Neve chattered on.

"Well, I heard they are all naked!" Anke interjected, her eyes wide with excitement.

Both girls giggled at the notion.

"I overheard two of the crew members talking this afternoon. They said that we should reach land in a couple of days but we will not go ashore till daylight and then leave immediately for the fort. The savages are dangerous and we have to move fast once we get on land."

Silence. The girls glanced at Penelope and Kent with pity as if they had spoken too much.

Penelope looked away quickly and began to wonder if the tales had been true after all. But, she would not think about that now. The wind was beginning to blow harder and made a whistle through the small open porthole. She went over and closed it. She could feel the mist of rain on her skin.

Mr. and Mrs. Zant returned. The rain had sent them back to the cramped room for shelter. Their two teenaged sons, Willem and Teunis, had pleaded with their father to let them stay on deck to help the crew with the rigging. They were fascinated with all things nautical and even talked of joining the Navy in a couple of years. Every night they taught their cabin mates a new nautical word and practiced tying knots in ropes. This was their chance to find out something of sea life before committing to it.

The inhabitants of the little room soon heard rain coming down harder and felt the *Kath* rocking more profusely. Side to side they all

CHAPTER 1

swayed so hard that standing was almost an impossibility. They all sat or lay on their bunks and hammocks trying not to think about the storm that swirled around them.

Penelope wiped Kent's brow and worked hard at not thinking about what was going on around her. She would just tend to her husband, that's all. No more talk of murder and savages. This storm would be no worse than the other rainstorms they had felt on this voyage she convinced herself. It would pass in just a little while.

It was dark now. Anke and Neve had fallen asleep. Wolter Zant held his huge Bible close to the lamp. Reading was making him nauseous with the movement going on, but just holding the book made him feel better. Mrs. Zant was trying to sew, but found the rocking of the room made it nearly impossible. Both parents were trying not to think about their two sons above deck. They were trying to let go and let them grow up. But, parents cannot turn off concern for their children.

At that moment, Willem and Teunis burst through the door. They were soaked to the bone and had a look of horror on their young faces. Their red hair was wet and wildly wrapped about their heads. Willem, being the oldest at nineteen, spoke first.

"Adam was just washed overboard!"

Adam was a young cabin boy who had befriended the Zant brothers on this voyage. This was his first working venture with his big brother, Dirk the boatswain. He was only fourteen and knew more about the sea life than the other boys. The Zant boys had been eager to learn what he knew and Adam had been just as eager to teach.

"How did that happen?" asked Mr. Zant in haste.

"Adam was going below deck because the captain told him to go down. When he was almost to the hatch a great wave peaked over the side and the boat tipped at the same time. Adam lost his footing and the wave carried him over." Willem stopped. He was too full of emotion to continue. He was almost to tears, but tried not to show them.

Teunis continued where Willem left off. "Dirk saw Adam

flapping abut in the waves behind the boat. He was struggling to stay afloat. Dirk grabbed a rope, tied it around his waist, and was about to jump in after him when Adam went under. We couldn't see him anymore. That's when the first mate grabbed him. He would not let Dirk go in after him. He told Dirk that he had already lost one good man tonight. He could not afford to lose another. It took two other crewmen to restrain Dirk."

"Poor Dirk. Adam was his brother. Where is Dirk now?" Mrs. Zant asked.

Fifteen-year-old Teunis could not answer anything else. He was beginning to shiver, not so much from the cold dampness of his body, but from the shock of seeing the anger of the ocean and his friend drown. His mother wrapped the two boys in blankets while their sisters got their brothers some dry clothes.

All the inhabitants of the tiny cabin remained silent, the shock still stinging the core of their being. Everyone had known the journey would be harsh. They had all heard the stories. No one just expected this kind of tragedy.

Penelope lay her head down beside her feverish husband and buried her head in the only dry spot on the bed. *Poor Adam* she thought. *Poor Dirk. What does the one left living think and feel? It must be harder on the one who could not help someone he loved.*

She looked at Kent. She was even more intent on seeing him through this now. She did not want to see the New World as a widow. She would not. She would will him into wellness. How ever loyal, how ever determined she had been at the beginning of Kent's sickness, she was even more so now. She wrapped her arms tighter around her invalid husband and held him on to him until she went to sleep.

Penelope was the first to wake the next morning. She looked out the porthole and saw that the sun was shining.

How deceiving the sunshine could be, she thought. *It shows no sign of last night's tragedy nor grief for Adam.*

Her cabin mates were still asleep. Mr. and Mrs. Zant looked at ease knowing their sons were safely in their bunks and not on deck.

CHAPTER 1

Anke and Neve were under their mutual blanket with only tufts of blonde hair showing. Willem and Teunis had kicked off their covers. They had not fallen asleep until just a couple of hours ago.

Penelope went to the galley for food. It seemed to her that the whole ship stank, even though the waves had thoroughly soaked everything last night. The smell was nauseatingly stale, rotting, and moldy. She decided then that when she got to shore she never wanted to experience that smell again.

The cook had toast and hardboiled eggs for the passengers. Penelope sat down and ate her toast and egg. She sipped her tea since she had never really cared for coffee. Kent liked coffee, however, so she would make sure her new home had plenty of it.

She asked the cook if she could have some broth to take to her husband. "That is the only sustenance I can get down him," she informed him.

"I have to make quite a bit of that lately. There are several passengers and crew members on the Binnacle list," he said as he handed her a cup of hot broth that he had already prepared. "The baron is not the only one eating broth these days."

"Thank you," she muttered. She took the cup from his large outstretched hand and walked back to her cabin. She held her head up and made each step more determined. He was going to eat something today she vowed.

When she got back to the cabin the Zant family was awake. Kent was even awake. He tried to smile at his bride, but his eyes were still weak.

"He awoke only a few minutes ago," said Mrs. Zant.

"How wonderful!" Penelope exclaimed. She turned to her now-awake husband and said, "I brought you some broth. You need to eat to build your strength."

He tried to sit up, but his weakened state would not allow it. The Zant boys came over to the bed and helped him prop his back, neck, and head up on the pillows Penelope had placed behind him. She noticed the difference in all the slender bodies around her. Kent's was slender and medium build, but his skin was still clammy and it hung on his bones, evidence of the weight loss. His fever had subsided somewhat, but his body was still hot. The boys' slim bodies were tall and muscular. Their white skin had turned ruddy and their freckles had gotten darker brown since they began their journey.

"I will get him healthy again and he will look just like them," she thought to herself.

"Well, let's go to the galley ourselves and get some breakfast," commanded the balding Mr. Zant. He was obviously the dominant force of the family. "We can't stay in here all day."

The family lined up to take their turn at exiting the small room, since only one at a time could get through the tiny door. Mrs. Zant, as usual, was the last in line. She reached over to her young friend and said, "I'll be right on deck if you need me. I will take my sewing up there."

"Thank you." Penelope had already decided that she would not need her. Kent was going to get well today. Mrs. Zant and everyone else knew better, but dared not say it to the young woman.

After the family was gone, Penelope lifted the cup to Kent's mouth. He sipped the brew slowly. Every swallow hurt his throat and he was too weak to even cough.

"I'm sor…" he began to speak.

She interrupted. "Shhhh. Don't speak right now. Just take your broth and get better. You are going to need your strength when we get to New Amsterdam. You still owe me a proper honeymoon." She smiled and winked at him.

He managed a small smile at her. He thought about what manner of wife he had. He was amazed at his choice. He had never made such a good decision or had such good luck. He thought how he must have used up all his luck by now.

After he had taken only half the cup of broth Kent fainted. His strength was gone and just the act of holding up his head had been too much for him.

Penelope helped him into a more comfortable position on the tiny makeshift bed and watched as the sweat beads again appeared on his face. The fever was back with a vengeance.

CHAPTER 1

She stayed with him all day, never leaving his side. Once more that afternoon he opened his eyes. He wouldn't eat, though. His words were whispered as he tried to touch his young beautiful wife's face. "I love you. I have loved you since I first saw you," he whispered.
"Shhh. We will talk when you get well."
She was quite surprised at his words. He LOVED her. She never knew how he felt. He had never said so. It must have been the fever talking.
The boat began rocking harder again. She got the same sick feeling that she had last night before Adam's terrible accident. Penelope braced herself for another horrible evening. She had seen young Adam's face in her nightmares all night. Would she see him again tonight? She just wouldn't sleep, that's all.
At nightfall the rain started again. The boat was tossed on every whim of the sea. Back and forth, increasingly it tilted.
By this time the Zant family had taken shelter in the cabin again. Mr. Zant had not allowed the boys to stay on deck this time. He did not want them to end up like Adam. There was no argument from either Willem or Teunis. They had decided that the Navy was not for them after all.
Crash. Crash. The waves were angry. Then, just before daybreak there was a terrible scraping and groaning of the *Kath*. It had hit the rocks off the coast of the New World. Everyone who was able ran to the porthole and took turns looking out. They could see land, but the boat was not floating. It was turned a quarter on its side resting on the large rocks with which it had collided.
"Abandon ship!" the first mate shouted.
The *Kath* only had three small boats on its side. There were three lifeboats for more people than five could hold. They were fortunate for now that the rocks held the boat up. But, there was no telling when the water would wash it from its resting-place. Everyone began to scamper around in a panic. The captain, who prided himself on his logic and discipline, called to the scared crew and passengers.
"We have plenty of time," said the captain in a calm voice. "Don't

panic. The crew will make three trips in each boat. We'll take the women and children first, the men next, and then we will see if we can salvage any of the cargo before we head on to the fort," the captain shouted.

Mrs. Zant, Anke, and Neve were in the first boat. They summoned Penelope, but she would not leave Kent.

"I'll come in another boat. Don't worry," she assured the ladies.

Penelope watched as the first two boats got smaller and smaller. Finally, they reached shore and the men of the crew on the lifeboats got out. The women and children were ordered to remain in the boat. Curiously, the men with their guns surveyed the area for quite a while before allowing the boat to be emptied.

"Baroness, we will help you get the Baron on the next boat. You don't have to leave him," Captain Danel Jacobson said to her.

"Thank you." She appreciated the help offered.

"Don't thank me yet," the captain said to her unemotionally. "There are savages on that shore that hate English and Dutch people, but most especially Dutch, anyone with blonde hair. We will not stay on that beach. As soon as we get everyone off this ship we will begin traveling on to New Amsterdam. I will not be responsible for having my passengers slaughtered when I can prevent it. If your husband is not able to walk we will have to leave him. I will not ask anyone to carry him. We only have enough time to get to the fort. I cannot afford for even one person to slow us down. I do not like the situation, but that is how it is. Even if he were my son I would have to make the same decision. I cannot loose everyone for the sake of one. I'm sorry."

"I...I...don't understand your cruelty and lack of compassion," she frowned at him. "Why must you get to the fort so quickly? Why can't someone help me carry him?"

Jacobson hated having to make this decision, but he went on with his unpleasant duty as if it did not bother him.

"Because, Baroness, the director general Kieft, in his infinite wisdom," he said sarcastically, "had an entire tribe of Indians slaughtered a few months ago over a few pigs. He didn't spare even

CHAPTER 1

the women or children. The savages are merely returning the favor. If we stay on that beach tonight, there is a good chance we will all be slaughtered by morning. You do see my position, don't you?"

"Yes," she said as she looked down at her feet. But, she quickly looked up again and hard at him. "But I'm just not sure who exactly the 'savages' are."

Ignoring the last comment, he said "I will have a fire built for your husband and get some shelter for him, but that is all I can do today. I will send someone back from the fort as soon as we arrive to help him. But, for today, I cannot carry him."

Quietly she answered "I understand."

"Good. You can come with the rescue party when they return for the Baron if you wish."

"No. I won't be coming back for him with a rescue party. I will be staying with him on the beach."

"I cannot allow you to do that. It is suicide. Can you not see that he most likely will die from fever during the night anyway? You would be risking your life for a dead man!"

Penelope suddenly found the will to stand up to a man. All those years of submitting to her father and never speaking back suddenly exploded within her. She stuck out her chin in defiance and said, "I WILL NOT LEAVE HIM."

Captain Jacobson could not believe his ears. He had never had someone defiantly stand up to him, and especially not a woman. She was crazy. She was not logical. It was just like a woman!

"Have it your way!" he shouted. He was tired of arguing with her. "I cannot make you understand what you are doing. They will kill you…or worse!" He leaned down to her so that his face was inches from hers and scowled at the pretty, slim, and contemptuous woman. He whispered diabolically "they do things to people I cannot even describe. You will wish you were dead long before they let you die. Baroness, I have seen the barbaric acts they have committed. You do not want to see that or be subjected to it, I assure you."

Penelope's eyes widened and her mouth went dry. After a long pause of looking directly into the captain's hardened eyes she stood firm. She gritted her teeth and said "I will not leave my husband. You have promised to help us get ashore. Very well. I will take care of Kent and myself until he is well or until help arrives."

The captain shook his head and instructed the first mate to load the Baron on to the next boat. The first mate looked at Penelope in amazement and hollered to the coxswain and two cabin boys with instructions. He could not believe that the captain had given the woman her way. Never had the captain given in to anyone.

Kent was loaded carefully into the lifeboat. By the time he was loaded, the whole crew knew the plan. They were especially kind to the couple and gentle during the row to shore. It only took a few minutes to get there, but it seemed much longer to Penelope since she and Kent were the objects of the stares of pity by the others.

Once on shore, one of the cabin boys began gathering wood for a fire. He gathered tree branches and made a lean-to. All this was done while the rest of the crew made the third and final trip back to the boat to salvage what supplies they could.

"Penelope, you cannot stay here," Mrs. Zant said as she held the young bride's arm. "It is not safe. I hate to tell you this, but I feel I must. It will not do any good for you to stay here. Kent is dying, my dear. I have seen fever like this before. Almost no one survives it. Now we have these terrible circumstances on top of everything else. I'm sorry, dear, but there is no chance he will survive. You must come with us."

Penelope looked at her older, wiser friend. The steely determination had not left her eyes.

"I will not leave my husband and I will not be a widow, not now, not here. You do what you must. Go with your family and get them to safety. I have to do what I must. I have to stay with my family."

Finally, after everyone was on shore and a few supplies had been salvaged, it was time for the herd of people to be on their way. Mrs. Zant had pleaded with Penelope as long as she could, but to no avail. Captain Jacobson was done with reasoning with this stubborn woman and did not look back. He just promised to send back a rescue team in his parting words to the baroness. The herd walked down the

CHAPTER 1

open beach to a clearing in the adjoining forest. The last person disappeared into the thicket as Penelope watched with her heart in her throat, pounding faster and faster. She looked back at Kent, realized the gravity of the situation and said out loud "What have I done?"

Chapter 2

Lady Deborah
Fall 1642

Lady Deborah Moody looked out the window of Director General Kieft's office and into the streets of New Amsterdam. She liked the hustle and bustle of the traffic and the smells of the bakery. This fort had many things to offer her, many things except the one thing she desperately wanted for her son and herself, the freedom to worship as she believed. How she missed her husband, rest his soul. He would have loved this new world adventure upon which they had embarked. She sighed and walked over to one of the two chairs in front of the large desk and sat down.

On the way to the director general's house this morning she had heard no less than ten different languages being spoken on the street. She loved the diversity of it all and had hoped that New Amsterdam would be the place for her, but it was not meant to be. The religious rules of man again overshadowed what she believed God's Word to say. Like other times before, her ideas of religious worship were not the same as the local church in charge and she, therefore, was told

CHAPTER 2

that her ideas were wrong without so much as a whiff of open-mindedness.

"He said he would be here at 10 O'clock," said Nicholas Stillwell, a land surveyor for the Dutch West India Company as he put his pocket watch back into his vest pocket. It was the only luxury he allowed himself.

Stillwell was forty-eight, tall, blonde, and very well built. He was impossibly meticulous about all business matters. Minute details were matters to be attended to, not left to themselves. Tardiness annoyed him, as did chaos, both of the disdainful traits the he believed Kieft embodied. Annoyed and almost apologetically, he said "sometimes the director is tardy."

"Yes," said Lady Moody, "I see."

Lady Moody sat up straight in her wooden chair. It seemed quite natural in her posture to do this as she was a lady of distinction and fine upbringing. She was a beautiful specimen of middle-aged womanhood with her long black hair meticulously pulled onto the top of her head without one single hair out of place. Her clothes were understated, yet she carried them well. She was not a large woman, yet she carried a large presence wherever she went, expecting—and getting—respect from everyone she met. She had an air of regality that few posses.

She studied the office of Director General William Kieft. It was as obnoxious as his reputation. The large wooden desk in the middle of the room was laden with papers, ink and quills in no order at all. The book shelves behind the desk did not hold books. Instead it held trophies and valuables, stolen or otherwise obtained. Kieft treasured them and wanted others to see the importance of himself. The fine furniture, imported from Holland, looked out of place in such a simple building.

"Well, I am glad to finally meet you, Lady Moody. I have heard much!" Director General Kieft said to her as he stormed into his office. He took her hand and, as a proper gentleman of fine upbringing would do, brought it up just below his face as he bowed, never allowing the hand to touch more than her glove.

Upon seeing Stillwell he turned his attention to the male dominance in the room and away from the lady. "Hello Stillwell. I understand you would like to inquire about some property."

Kieft was a rotund man with a put on smile and dressed in all the finery that a man of his position required, and then some. His carriage was one of self-importance and he had the habit of holding his head a little too high so as to look down on those of less position and status. He had a reputation for holding others to a code of morality that he himself sometimes failed to keep, especially when no one was looking. He was sometimes called William the Testy because he was so disagreeable. Most people were happy when things were quiet. Not Kieft. He was not content unless things were stirred up.

"Hello. Yes, you see..." began Stillwell.

"Thank you, sir, I can speak for myself," began Lady Deborah Moody. She looked at him rather firmly, but kindly, and then over to Kieft who was behind his fine desk by now. Stillwell looked back at her, raised one eyebrow, and offered her a nod. He was obviously not used to being admonished by a woman, but had learned that the best way to work with Lady Moody was to let her have her way. "I am interested in chartering a plot of land that you offer on the patroon system."

Lady Deborah had already studied and familiarized herself with the patroon system that the Dutch West India Company was offering. It looked like just the thing for the people that were with her who might not have as much money as others, but wanted to make a start for themselves. It worked on a plan that allowed the patroon, or leaser, to pay a portion of the land's profits over a span of ten years, gaining equity on each payment. If the payments were not made the Company would repossess the property. The system was much like a mortgage only it allowed the purchaser to make yearly payments based on the productivity of the land, rather than monthly payments. This system could be beneficial for both parties. It made sure the property was put to use and settled which made the property value of surrounding plots go up, thereby being prosperous for the Company. It also allowed the purchaser to pay as he went rather than having to

CHAPTER 2

have all the money at one time.

Kieft had never done business with a woman before, at least not business that one talked about. He sat there for a second or two to take in the events of the moment. Perhaps, this lady was merely the one with the money and needed to feel her importance. After all, it was well known that she was a lady of nobility and nobility always held a high self esteem. *Very well,* he thought, *I will indulge the rich widow if that means selling land.*

"Ah yes, on the tithe system. You do understand that the system means that the patroons must pay the West India Company a tithe from any product grown for the next ten years? After that, the land becomes the property of the patroon. If the debt is not paid, the property reverts back to our company."

"Yes, that is my understanding," said Lady Moody.

"Very well. I think I know just exactly the property that would suit you" he said as he shuffled his papers on his desk, looking for a map.

"No. I would like the land that is across the bay from New Amsterdam, the one that was recently acquired from the Canarsie, a place called Bruijkleen." She produced her own map and handed it across the table to him. "The land that is mapped here, this part of Bruijkleen," she said as she pointed to the area at the southeast end of the map. She was getting down to business because she had already studied and discussed with experts her plan and she was not about to get sidetracked by this little man.

"Oh, I see." Kieft gave a sharp, contemptuous look at Stillwell who had given her the map, knowing full well that Stillwell was enjoying the director general's uncomfortable situation too much.

Stillwell grinned. He was English, as was Lady Moody. Kieft was Dutch. Stillwell, although working for the Dutch, still held the opinion that the English were superior, especially to this man whom he held in great disdain. How he did enjoy seeing a woman get the best of Kieft!

Kieft studied the map for a moment and then spoke slowly. "Well, that is a good choice for a settlement, but who will be leading this charter?"

"I will, of course." Lady Moody looked directly into the director's eyes with steely determination as firm as any man's. She was annoyed that he had thought someone else would lead, but his notion had been expected.

"But, Lady Moody, you don't…" his voice trailed off and he at once glanced over to Stillwell who was standing back and to the side of her. Stillwell shot a look back, cocked his head to the side, and shrugged as if to say "your turn and you are on your own."

"Sir, I am perfectly capable of leading a settlement. I have had experience leading others for a long time now, first in England, then in Massachusetts, and now here in New Amsterdam. I should like to think that one's gender has nothing to do with one's leadership capabilities in the matter of land acquirement. I have taken the liberty of having Mr. Stillwell and associates survey the property and draw this map. We have divided the settlement into parts in a way that I believe will be most beneficial to everyone. I have recruited several families ready to go with me. I believe I have already done the ground work for this new settlement. I merely need your approval for the charter and to inquire of a few other details" she said matter-of-factly, as if she had had this type of discussion many times before.

William Kieft was left speechless for a moment. He had never met such a woman. She was forthright, bold, infuriating, and down right charming simultaneously, exactly as her preceding reputation had claimed. He looked at her for a moment and believed that she probably could start a settlement on her own and probably would with or without his approval. She had won his admiration by her fortitude and outspokenness.

Finally, after a short silence he spoke. "What other details?"

"There is the business of religion," she began. "I am told that Dutch settlements are required to hold allegiance to the Dutch Reformed Church. I would like for this settlement to have no such allegiance. I believe that each person should have the freedom to worship as he believes without the church of the government intervening. It is a purely private matter. The ones who will be going

CHAPTER 2

with me espouse the same belief. We do not want or need the Dutch Reformed Church dictating our lives to us. We want the liberty to worship as we see fit."

There it was; the "freedom of religion" thing again. Kieft had figured that somehow she would bring religion into the deal. He had heard that she had done that everywhere else she had been, never satisfied with the churches that were established in the locations she settled, never wanting to baptize babies, always wanting to change things, always challenging the men. This woman had even dared the church elders on the established custom of infant baptism, believing one had to be an adult to make the decision rather than having the parents make it for their children! Why, even her own son had to wait until he was old enough to say he wanted to be baptized before she would allow it!

What was it with these religious people? They were never satisfied. Old Parson Bogardus, the ordained minister in the church down the street had come over with Kieft on the same ship. He was never satisfied with anything Kieft had done. He had once called Kieft a child of the devil to his face. The old parson was so undaunted by Kieft that after the director general had caused trouble between some of the traders Bogardus had become so angry that he yelled to Kieft publicly that if he did not behave himself he would give him such a shake from the pulpit next Sabbath it would make him shake like a bowl of jelly. The only thing that Kieft ever did right for the old man was to have the new church built and install bells taken in a battle from Puerto Rico in the belfry.

It was a well known fact that the Dutch West India Company insisted, nay compelled, its patroons to be part of the Dutch Reformed Church because it was part of the agreement packages. It was just like a woman to want to start changing everything. First she wanted to start and lead a settlement, and if that wasn't enough, now she wanted to start changing the rules on religion, too. This widow wanted to change all of the status-quos!

But, Kieft also knew he was in hot water with his employers for not moving the settlements along fast enough. He casually got up from his desk and walked over to his window to think for a moment. He had to get new settlements started and soon or lose his very comfortable position of director general. There were already those in his administration who wanted him gone. The aborigines, as he called them, had messed up everything. They had begun to figure out that he was cheating them and fought back, scaring off any white person that might be interested in a new settlement. That is, everyone except this woman and the few that would follow her.

Perhaps she was not aware of the dangers. If she wasn't, then he would let her find out the hard way. If she was aware of the dangers then she was braver than he imagined. Either way, she got her settlement and he got the boss off his back.

After a moment he spoke. "You don't know what you are asking. I am already going out on a limb here by letting a WOMAN lead a settlement. You want me to go even further out on that limb by allowing you to deny the Dutch Reformed Church?"

"I don't consider that you are going out on a limb. I look at it as you are an enlightened leader, a person not afraid of challenges, a great pioneer," she said in a persuasive voice, knowing that his oversized ego could not resist these compliments. She had dealt with men like this before and knew the way to make them come around to her way of thinking. They merely needed compliments, not confrontation at this stage of negotiations. It was a skill she had acquired when she had dealt with other, less obstinate scoundrels.

It worked. He liked the sound of "enlightened leader." He would be doing something no one else had ever done, letting a woman lead a settlement. Its success would mean more money for his coffers. And, if it failed, it would only mean that he had at least tried to make a go of something new and different. After all, it was a woman leading for God's sake! Failure would be expected. He would not lose either way.

Still, he had to make a show of determination. "What kind of religion do you propose to instill there?"

"None," she said firmly. "Worship may be done in the homes if the people want so that there will be no established religion. I want

CHAPTER 2

a community of religious tolerance, not religious stagnation. I do not want religious persecution at this settlement and the only way to have the tolerance is to do away with the government-sanctioned church. This does not mean that I do not want religion there. No, exactly the opposite, I want each person to have the liberty to worship as his own will sees fit. I have had enough of having another's religion force-fed to me. Hopefully, in this settlement I will finally have the freedom I have so long desired. I do, however, have plans for a church building on one of the town blocks. Of course, it will be non-denominational so that all may use it if they desire. It will not be government ordained."

"And what do you propose to name this settlement?" asked Kieft trying to get off the subject of religion fearing a sermon from this woman could easily arise at any moment.

"Gravesend," she said with a smile after a pause. It had just occurred to her that her voice had become somewhat louder when she spoke about her passion for religious freedom. She brought it back down to a refrained quality. "It was a place in England that I loved to visit as a child. It sort of gives a feeling of home to me."

Stillwell, amazed at realizing that Lady Deborah had just persuaded the director general to let her have her settlement and that she had gotten so far, finally spoke up with a voice of reason on a minute detail that had been neglected. "What about the natives? Haven't you had problems of recent with them?"

He was right to be concerned. There had been an outbreak of attacks. Stillwell himself had even had to abandon his northern tobacco plantation after experiencing the attacks of the Indians. He had seen the hostilities and knew the gravity of their presence.

The natives had been regrouping and recruiting other tribes to join in their war against the white man. Stillwell knew this from the reports that his soldier friends had given him. Several battles had taken place in recent months with atrocities on both sides. There had been a war over something as trivial as pigs and uprisings were going on all over. Each time the natives got the brunt end and they were getting tired of the white men. Things would not be pretty as long as

Kieft's idea of negotiations with the Indians was to kill them all. He wanted Lady Moody to have all the facts before she made this decision. He had tried talking to this headstrong woman before she came to see Kieft, but to no avail. She knew what she wanted and was not going to stop until she got there.

"Well, I would not worry about those aborigines," Kieft puffed up. "We have quieted the small skirmishes that some of their rogues have provoked. There is no need for alarm now because we have scouted the area and found that the aborigines in that area do not have access to firearms or firewater. It should be perfectly safe for this settlement."

"But, what about…" Stillwell tried to protest.

"Ahh, it is nothing to worry about." Kieft interrupted and then cleared his throat. He looked hard at Stillwell and said "We should have everything completely under control in just a few months. The remnants of the tribes are relatively harmless now because we have already cleared the area of the dangerous ones. You have nothing to worry about. I will even send a protective detail escort with you to get the settlement established when the time comes. How does that sound? Is that fair?"

"Yes, very good indeed," Lady Moody said as she picked up her coat and purse. "Your new patroons and I will return when the paperwork is ready for the signing of the charter for the new land. Good day, sir, and thank you."

Stillwell helped her with her coat and gave a hard, I-know-what-you-just-did look to Kieft. Kieft grinned and opened the door for the two to exit.

"I will attend to it and see you. You do realize this will take some time. I will let you know when the papers are ready," Kieft said as Stillwell and Lady Moody went through the door.

He shut it behind them and congratulated himself on a deal that could not lose. He rather liked Lady Moody, but not enough to jeopardize any deal she might want to make. Not many women would have the fortitude to even ASK for a charter, let alone go after it with the determination that she had shown. Not many men would

CHAPTER 2

have taken the steps to go ahead and have it surveyed and divided before it was even agreed upon either. He almost hoped the settlement was a success for her sake.

Chapter 3

Stranded on the beach

Penelope looked at her surroundings. The beautiful beach was quite the liar. It did not look at all dangerous at this moment, even though it had just proven how lethal it could be. She had been around the sea for most of her life, having lived her life in the harbor town of Amsterdam. Granted, she had observed it only from the land, up until the past few weeks. But, she hoped she knew enough to at least get them through the next couple of days.

She puttered around trying to keep herself busy so that she wouldn't have to think. *Are there really savages around here?* she thought. Then she answered herself, *Of course not. They were all just scared of tall tales. Besides, if someone comes along I will just reason with them and show that I am not a threat.*

Penelope went on with her nesting. She made sure Kent was out of the sun and comfortable in the lean-to. She put another couple of sticks on the fire, even though it really didn't need it. She dug through the basket that the cook had left for her. It looked like enough food for a couple of days or maybe more. He even left a piece of cake that he had left over from yesterday's lunch. The sticks that the crew had

CHAPTER 3

collected from the thicket would keep the fire for several days. She had plenty of blankets. Their clothes and things could not be salvaged from the ship, but at least she had a few supplies to last until she got to the fort and she had managed to get Kent into his fine coat and breeches before the cabin boys had come to carry him to the lifeboat.

"Well, nothing to do but wait," she said to the now-comatose Kent. She still thought he was sleeping. There was no movement or even a groan from him in six hours. His breathing had become labored, but his chest *was* moving up and down. That was enough for her. She would not let him die. Her strength would sustain both of them.

Night came and she covered both Kent and herself in the extra blankets. Penelope watched as the tide slowly lifted the tiny-looking *Kath* from its rocky resting-place and lured it out away from safety. It went down without any great fanfare or noise, just the lap, lap, lap of the water licking the shore. The hull became smaller and smaller. Then, the boatswain chair went down and finally the crow's nest. For over an hour it slowly sank until she could no longer see any part of the mast. The full moon reflected on the water and made the show even more visually dramatic. She thought about how odd it was that she felt loss for something she considered to be a prison.

Finally, sleep came. She dreamt of Kent and their children, of flowers and crops, and of friends around her. It was a nice dream. It had been so long since she had fully slept that she let herself sink as far from reality as she could. Her brain must have thought she was on holiday. For the first time in months she was free.

She was startled from her lovely holiday by screams unlike any she had ever heard. They were shrill and cold. Her eyes flew open just in time to see a young man with black hair only on the center of his head jump on top of her, grab her right arm and hold it above her head. Instinctively she brought her left arm over in front of her body almost as a shield. She saw only a glimpse of a strange looking axe. He slashed quickly. She felt a sting on her stomach and her left arm. She wanted to scream but her voice betrayed her so that she could not make a sound. The movements around her were happening so fast that her shocked brain could not comprehend the events.

Penelope looked over to Kent who had been resting on the blanket. He was almost decapitated and he had only a bloody mess where hair once was. An older, strange looking, nearly naked man stood over him. The reality of what was going on was beginning to sink in. Before she could even fight back, the man on top of her grabbed her long blonde locks and pulled her head back so hard that her neck felt like it would break. He took his strange looking axe and did something to the top of her head. She collapsed without a whimper. All went dark around her.

When she finally awoke it was night again. Her arm, head, and abdomen stung. Blood was everywhere. Was it hers or Kent's? It was a mixture of both. She saw his lifeless bald bloody body in the sand near the water. He had been stripped of his clothes as if their attackers wanted to continue the humiliation. The tide was coming in so that half of his body was in the ocean.

It hurt to think. The pain in her head pounded and stung all at the same time. She reached up to her head to hold it as one does when the pain is so severe. The touch caused the pain to become excruciating. There was also something else. She felt no hair in the center part of her head. Her head was wet and sticky and her touch caused the stinging to intensify. When she pulled her right hand back down to her eyes she saw that it was full of blood and hair. That is when she found her voice. The scream that bellowed from her lungs started at her toes and worked its way upward. She felt as though the voice was someone else's—not hers.

The effort of forcing that scream caused her stomach to hurt. She looked down to see that her body was almost entirely covered in blood. The rag that used to be her dress clung to her body, wet and sticky. She tried to move her left arm, but it would not. She took her bloody right hand, put it on her stomach and felt a wound that had something trying to come out of it. It was her intestines! She pushed the exposed part back into the gaping wound and held it there with her one good bloody hand.

CHAPTER 3

It hurt to think, but she had to try. She wondered what had happened, why those men attacked them. As they had been sleeping, they obviously were not threatening to anyone. Then she remembered what Captain Jacobson had said.

"…An entire tribe…slaughtered…hate blonde hair…retaliation."

"We killed their people so they kill ours," Penelope said to herself. "They thought I was dead so they left us both here."

She tried to move in spite of the pain. She did not have to gather her dress because there was little left of it. Only her undergarments were whole. She did not know why they had not humiliated her sexually, but at least she had been spared something.

She crawled slowly, only inches at a time, to the water's edge where her dead husband had been dragged by his attackers. Kent was not in pain. She could not help him, but she could not pity him either. She felt anger towards him for bringing her here, for getting sick, and for leaving her. Hadn't she been a good wife to stay with him? How could he have let this happen? The anger and resentment was followed immediately by guilt for having those feelings. She knew full well that he could not help his illness or the attack or that he was dead and she was not. But, emotions do not often follow logic. They have their own agenda and their carrier must submit to them or suppress them. Either way a body hurts. She hurt physically, emotionally, and now spiritually. She saw no reason to suppress anything at this point. She was alone, injured, and unknown things surrounded her.

"God, please just let me die, too!" she screamed. It was not so much that she wanted to join Kent because of love, she only wanted out of the pain. Death would be a welcomed relief to her.

She thought about Dirk and how he felt when he could not save Adam. At this moment she understood the emptiness of that helpless feeling. But, Dirk had others to help him with the grief. She had no one and was severely wounded, too.

Penelope thought about her father and how that he would most likely be praying right now. She wanted to pray but she had no words. She began to think that God had abandoned her and that He did not even remember her enough to let her die. How could she pray to someone who let her live? These thoughts made her heart hurt as well as her head.

The pounding inside her brain deafened her. She looked around. Where could she find shelter? She knew better than to stay on the beach again tonight. The open unprotected beach offered nothing for her. She hated the thought of it, but she was going to have to drag herself to the wooded area that adjoined it and try to find some shelter there.

Putting her good hand on her stomach wound to keep her insides in, she tried to stand. Her knees began to buckle at the task they were asked to perform, but they did not fail her. Little step by little step she made her way to the thick part of the forest. Her one good stroke of luck was that the full moon put out enough light so that she could at least see some of where she was going.

Finally, the trek to the forest was complete. The walk felt endless, but in reality was only a few yards. She fell to her knees and the impact of the fall caused the stomach wound to protrude. Her hand pushed the escaping intestines back to their proper place. She looked around for somewhere to lie down. She would need a few more steps to look for a good spot.

Penelope found the strength to rise again and stagger a few more yards. She caught site of a hollow tree with just enough hole for her weary body to prop up in. "Just a few more steps," she encouraged herself.

Upon reaching her destination, she pulled herself into the tree. Sweat beaded on her face; at least she thought it was sweat. In reality it was a mixture of sweat and blood. Being careful not to let the bark or anything else touch her wounded head, she leaned herself back against the trunk. Exhaustion overcame her and she slept.

The nightmares pursued her. Adam, Dirk, Kent, and her father crept into her brain. They presented themselves as acts in a play. Adam screamed for help, but none came. His screams were drowned by Dirk's keening. He wanted to die, too, but he could not. The second act followed with Kent. She kept seeing him put her on a tiny

CHAPTER 3

dingy and push her out into the ocean as he sat on shore and waved to her. His body grew smaller and smaller. She was left entirely alone in a small boat in the middle of the ocean. The curtain came down and the third act came. Her father preached to her about God and His love. He pounded the pulpit and preached and preached and preached in an unmerciful and fearful tone.

A sharp pain on what was left of her tender scalp awakened Penelope. A small twig was tangled in her matted hair and reached out to scrape the open wound. Pulling it out became an impossible task with only one hand. Her left arm was so severely hacked that the muscles would not work. It hung by her body in uselessness. She broke off the small twig and brushed it away from the sore spot as best she could

The sun's rays beamed through the leafy filter of the forest. It gave full view today for what the partial one had been last night. Trees were everywhere and so was the underbrush. She saw briars, vines, and sticky things as one with open wounds to protect would.

Desperately she wanted to just sleep, to die. But, curiosity fueled her eyelids to stay open. This New World was not like the description that Kent and Reverend Thomson had given her. It was not just like Amsterdam and there were certainly no opportunities for her here, especially since she was now a widow.

"O Sacred Head now wounded..." she sang in delirium. "How does that song go?" Penelope laughed a sarcastic little laugh to herself at the irony of thinking of that song.

She knew she had to move around or face becoming weaker. She forced herself out of the hollow tree and into a standing position. Every muscle in her body ached and she reeked of sweat mixed with blood. She decided to go back to the beach to see if there was anything left in the food basket or if a rescue party had returned for her. Holding her guts in, she slowly shuffled toward the ocean being careful to avoid anything pointy that might touch her wounds or catch on her matted hair.

When she finally reached the clearing she saw Kent's body still out there. The sea had not carried it out in compassion, but bloated it beyond recognition as if to get in its own jab of humiliation to the couple. Penelope suddenly realized how badly she smelled so she decided to wash herself in the ocean, forgetting about the salt in the water. She went farther down the shoreline away from Kent.

She waded into the clear blue-green water up to her thighs and took her good arm and splashed onto her bloody garments and body, hoping to rid herself of some of the foul odor. Upon the salt water hitting her open stomach wound she screamed. She would not dare try to dip her tender head into it. Near fainting she pulled herself out of her torture bath back onto the shore.

After resting a while to let the pain subside, she remembered the food basket. Dragging herself up again, Penelope struggled back to the ruins of their lean-to. She looked around the remains of the makeshift camp for any sign of the basket. There was none. It was gone, either taken by her attackers or by wild animals. At any rate, she had no provisions. There was only one blanket left that was not covered in blood. The others had been soaked. She took it, left the camp spot, and did not turn back.

Penelope heard her stomach rumble and felt her tongue getting thicker from thirst. She needed food and water, but where, how? There was no fresh water to be found. Trying not to stumble and being extra careful not to bump her head on any low-hanging twigs, she stumbled to her hollow tree. There were mushrooms growing around it. Dew was still on some of the leaves in the underbrush.

She had no choice other than starvation. Falling to the ground, Penelope leaned over and took a bite of the mushroom. It had a musty taste, but it filled her stomach. She did not care if the mushrooms were poisonous. The only thing she could do for water was to lick dew from the leaves around her, which she did.

So much the better, she thought. *If I die from eating them it will be to my benefit.*

Still holding her stomach wound so that her intestines would not protrude, she leaned gently back into the shelter of her tree. The bark pricked her sore head so she took her hand away from her stomach and tore off some of her undergarment and tied it around her head.

CHAPTER 3

Then, she was able to lean back against the tree. She took her blanket, wrapped it around herself, and tried to get as comfortable as she could.

Penelope succumbed to sleep that had trailed her after fighting it as long as she could so as to stay away from her nightmares. Hearing Adam's screams, Dirk's cries, and her father's voice was more than she could bear. The reality of loneliness was bad enough without the even lonelier feeling she had when Kent pushed her out into the ocean. She hated dreams. She hated reality. She could feel insanity creeping up.

This time fate had pity on her. She slept the rest of the day and all night soundly. No movement, no dreams, and no sounds came from her, only sleep that took her far away into nothingness. Blackness surrounded her and it felt better than where she had been.

The next morning she awoke to a drip, drip, drip around her. It was a gentle rain, not like the storms in the past few days, but caressing and soothing. The sound of it falling was like a lullaby to her ears, a soft whisper to her soul. She held her dirty hand outside of the tree and let the rain catch in the cup of her palm. She pulled her hand back in and drank. Penelope did this repeatedly, never really getting enough to drink, but having enough to quench some of the thirst. She removed some of the rags that she had on and let the rain rinse the dirt as much as it could.

The moisture of the ground was conducive to mushroom growth so she had more of them to eat. She did not like the taste, but knew that they would keep her alive. Dying would be a welcomed thing, but she did not want to die by starvation. Standing was harder to do now, so she just laid her body on the ground so that her mouth would be more level to the mushrooms. She ate the ones closest to her mouth and closed her eyes again. Exhaustion overcame her.

The next three days were blurred. Exhaustion and blood loss caused her to sleep more and more. When she was awake, she tried to listen for search parties, but none came. Had they found Kent's body? Did they think she was dead, too? Had they even come back for them as Captain Jacobson had promised to do?

Her mind played tricks. She heard voices, but no one was there. She had conversations with people that lived in Amsterdam. They were real to her and so much the better. It was better to be crazy than alone. She never questioned the insanity. She rather needed it.

Every now and then Penelope would try to pray. She remembered parts of her father's sermons she had heard through the years and tried to concentrate on them. She had accepted Christ as her Savior when she was a young girl, but church had really only been a source of social involvement for her. Penelope had thought of her salvation only casually in the last few years. Although she had committed to Christ, she had never really *needed* Him before now.

"Why don't you let me die?" Penelope cried as she prayed. Tears came fully and freely. "I don't know what you want from me. I have tried to be a good daughter and a good wife. Now, I am here and I am alone. My arm is useless and my body hurts in every place. You have no plan for me."

Reverend Thomson's voice rang in her ears. "Faith, faith is the fruit of the true believer!" His voice was so loud. "Faith is the substance of things hoped for, the evidence of things not seen, so Paul tells us! Paul knew of trials and he knew of faith. Be like Paul!"

She had heard his sermons all her life, but never really thought about the suffering part of the commitments he preached about. She tried to remember details of the speeches. Her mind wandered back to an earlier verse from Hebrews that her father quoted so often. "It is a fearful thing to fall into the hands of the living God." Now she knew what that meant.

Wasn't Paul shipwrecked? Wasn't he beaten? Yet, he never failed in his faith. Why is it different for me? Why should I fail in my faith? How did he manage to keep his faith in his suffering? Did he suffer less or more than I? she thought. *Is this the love of a merciful God—to let me die this way? I see no plan for my life.*

Penelope's head hurt and the concentration on her anger was becoming more difficult. Her brain could not hold any one thought for long at a time and she thought she was beginning to go insane permanently. The pain was becoming unbearable, nauseatingly so,

CHAPTER 3

but to vomit would mean the pressure would push her intestines through the open wound again. She could not let that happen.

Her mind was beginning to play tricks on her. She thought she had heard a dog bark close by, but she had not seen a dog since she had arrived. As the disabled woman tried to force her brain to study on this she felt a cold wet nose on her hand. It nudged her. There, wagging its tail back and forth forcefully was a big black dog. He barked a few times, sniffed her, and then began licking her wounds. He alternated between barking, sniffing, and licking for the next couple of minutes.

She heard more rustling. Was it more dogs or maybe even wild animals? She forced herself to look up to see the two men who loomed over her. Their appearance was similar to that of her attackers a few days ago. Their heads were trimmed to look as if they had black manes in the center. One man was young and the other man looked as if he could have been the first's father. They wore leather covering as pants and strange necklaces adorned their bodies. The old man had an animal coat of some kind on his back. Penelope recognized the weapons they carried because they had the same kind of axes as the attackers had used to kill Kent and mangle her.

Thinking that God had finally answered her prayers for death, Penelope crawled slowly out of the hollow tree. She stopped on her knees outside of her shelter and looked up at the younger man. Then, bowing her head to show the torn scalp to her executor and to signify her willingness to die, she prayed for forgiveness from Jesus in her moment of death.

The young man looked at this shattered white woman with compassion. He saw the bloody arm that hung to her side, her stomach wound that she held with her other arm, the maggot infected scalp, and the look of hopelessness in her eyes. He reached across his waste, pulled the tomahawk from its resting place in his belt, and drew back to slay his willing victim.

At that moment the older man grabbed his arm and shook his head. The young man slowly withdrew his stance. Penelope looked up wondering what was taking so long. She saw pity in the two men's eyes and this bewildered her. She could not imagine that these "savages" would know what pity was. She pointed to her neck and to the axe that was still in the young man's hand.

The young man looked back at the old one as if to ask "why not?" The old one again shook his head. They spoke to each other in a language she did not understand. She did, however, understand their body language. The young man was arguing for her death, the old one for her life. Upon seeing that they were going to let her live, Penelope tried to protest by climbing to her feet, but her body would not let her. She fainted at the attempt, but the old man caught her. He took his animal coat and wrapped Penelope's frail bloody body in it. Then he put her across his shoulder as gently as he could. The trio left the wooded area and went northward on the beach without any words spoken.

Chapter 4

Where am I?

Penelope awoke to the muffled sounds of people that seemed far away from her. She could hear them speaking and laughing, but she could not understand the language. It wasn't English and it wasn't Dutch. It almost sounded French, but not quite. She still had not opened her eyes. The sounds had merely crept in through her ears and stirred her brain.

When she finally forced her eyes to open, she saw a middle-aged grey haired woman sitting beside her mat on the floor sewing some kind of animal skin. There were no chairs in the room, but there were the most colorful blankets that she had ever seen lying around. She was in a hut of some kind that was made of sticks. It was unlike the stone and wood houses she was used to.

She moaned as her body stirred and the grey-haired lady noticed her. She smiled at Penelope and spoke, but Penelope could not understand her. She noticed that most of the lady's teeth were missing and the ones that did remain were in poor condition. But, she was not frightening or ugly. She had put down her sewing and was trying to comfort Penelope. She spoke in dulcet tones and patted

Penelope's hand in a soothing motion. Although the words were confusing, the body language was not. This lady had helped her and would not harm her.

Penelope moved her right arm, her good arm, slowly. It was so heavy that she could barely lift it. She put it across her stomach wound, remembering the pain. She felt something hard across the wound. Looking down, she saw that there was a type of red substance on it, sealing some sort of stitching that was done to her skin. Upon further investigation, she found that it was tree resin. It had covered the stitches, kept her skin together and her intestines in tact.

She reached up to feel her wounded head. The maggots were gone and the scab was healing. There was some sort of salve on it that was oily to her fingers. Her left arm moved only slightly. It was healing, but it was somewhat smaller now than her right one. Obviously, she had been well cared for, but she did not know for how long she had been there.

The grey-haired lady said something to her and disappeared out the door. Penelope thought how oddly this woman was clothed. She had on a long dress that went down to about mid calf with breeches underneath. She had beads around her neck and strange animal hide type shoes. Penelope had never seen a woman dressed in this manner. It was different, yet beautiful, so colorful. The woman had brown skin, like her attackers…and her saviors.

Penelope laid her head back against the mat. She had little strength to chase her thoughts, let alone after this woman who had just exited the hut. How long had she been there, a day, a week, several weeks? How easy it is to loose track of time. The short term memory was blurred. After a few moments, the lady returned with the old man that had stopped the young one from euthanizing her.

"Hello," the man said to her. "Sleep long time. Bet-ter?" His speech was slow and studied. He was not comfortable with the English language.

Penelope nodded. At that moment she thought of her bald head and tried to lift her blanket to cover it, but the blanket was too heavy for her weakened state.

CHAPTER 4

The man knew she was trying to cover herself and said "Will heal. Talk later."

With that he left the hut. The nice woman stayed with her. She spoke again in soothing, soft, lullaby-like tones, so much so that before long Penelope was asleep again.

Later that evening, Penelope awoke. The same lady was still with her. She had brought some kind of broth. Penelope lifted her head slightly to take the nourishment from this woman, this stranger. The liquid tasted different from anything she had ever experienced. She drank from the clay bowl as much as she could, then let her head ease back down.

"Thank you," Penelope said to the woman.

The woman smiled at her and said something. Penelope did not know what she said, but it sounded nice. It was relaxing. She was soon back asleep.

The next morning she awoke to the lady and the old man standing over her.

"Up. Up now," the old man said.

He turned and called to the two young women dressed similarly to the old woman just outside the entrance. They came inside. Together, the three women helped Penelope slowly stand to her feet and keep the blanket around her body as she was naked underneath and they sensed her embarrassment. She was woozy, but she was able to stand.

She felt the weight of the stares of the two young women. They were looking at her wounded head. They looked at each other with a sympathetic, yet disgusted horror at the scar. Penelope instinctively tried to reach toward it with her good hand. Embarrassed, she looked down. She could not understand their words, but she understood the humiliation she felt upon their inspection of her head.

The old woman said something harsh to the young women. Their facial expressions faded and they left. She turned to Penelope and held out her hand as if to say that she would help her walk. Penelope liked this woman and immediately trusted her. They didn't need the verbal language. This wise woman used the language of kindness to bridge the barriers.

Then, the man pointed to himself and said "Owehela." Then he pointed to her and grunted.

"Oh," she thought, "he wants to know my name."

She pointed to herself and said "Penelope."

The man pointed to himself and said "O-we-he-la" again. Then he pointed to Penelope and said "Pe-ne-lo-pe."

She nodded.

"Teach Owehela white talk." He pointed to himself. This was said as a command, not as a question or suggestion. This man was obviously a leader who was respected, and quite comfortable with giving orders.

Penelope did not understand at first. Then, after looking curiously at the tall brown man for a moment, she looked back at her new surrogate mother. The kind woman smiled and nodded. The idea soon hit her that her looks had gotten her into this predicament and how this moment was all so ironic. First, her blonde hair had gotten her scalped and left for dead. Now, it had saved her. This man had saved her life so that she could teach him English.

"Oh," Penelope said after she realized what he wanted. "You want me to teach you how to speak English."

The man nodded. "En-glaash," he said. "Need En-glaash…trade." He held out shells to accentuate what he was saying. "Wampum trade."

"I see. You need to speak the language so you will be able to trade with the English.

She looked down at her feet for a moment. No one had really ever wanted her to teach anything before and she thought about how strange this whole situation was. If she had heard this tale told by someone else, she would not believe it. Yet, these events were happening to her, and they were very real.

Penelope looked up at the tall man and nodded. "Yes, I will try."

The man smiled. His teeth were white and straight. How they shone against his brown skin when he smiled, she thought. Although he looked similar to those who attacked her, he had a different

CHAPTER 4

countenance, a different spirit. His mannerisms commanded respect and his mercy invited her friendship.

She had been standing for several minutes and her legs began to give way. The lady took a firm hold of Penelope and gently helped her back to her bed. Penelope's head was swimmy and her ears rang. Little flickers of light filled her eyes as everything went dark. Through the darkness she heard the woman's voice. This time the woman was singing softly. Penelope relaxed and allowed the darkness to consume her once again. That voice, it was almost hypnotic.

Several hours later Penelope awoke to wonderful smells. The lady looked at her and got up from where she had been tending vigil with the patient. She went outside and soon came back in with a clay bowl of food. As she came nearer to Penelope she put down the bowl and gently helped her sit upright. When Penelope was sufficiently balanced, the lady handed the full bowl to her. It had some meat in it and strange looking vegetables of some kind. Penelope didn't care what it was, it smelled wonderful.

She looked around for a spoon. There was none. How she desperately wanted some of this delicious smelling food. She looked over to the woman and was just about to ask for a utensil when the lady looked back at her with her own bowl in her hand. She smiled at Penelope and held up the bowl to her own mouth. With her fingers she picked up some of the contents and put it into her mouth. Then, she pointed to Penelope's mouth and said, "mitsi, mitsi!"

Penelope understood. She was to eat the food with her hand. Her left arm was still not working well, so she placed the bowl in her lap. With her right hand she picked up some of the food and put it in her mouth. How wonderful it tasted! These new tastes melted in her mouth and she savored each bite. It was so good in fact that after a while she didn't mind that she was eating with her hand.

It was only after Penelope had eaten nearly the whole bowl of food that she noticed that everyone in the hut was watching her. She blushed with embarrassment. She thought that she must look a site, this bald-headed, mangled woman eating like an animal! And, there were new people in the hut now; two young boys, another older lady, and the young man who had wanted to put her out of her misery.

She stopped, still holding a portion of food in her hand at her mouth and looked around the room. She then saw that they were all grinning at her, not in a mocking way, but in a pleasant welcome-to-the-family, we-are-glad-you-like-it kind of way. She looked down at her bowl, shrugged, and grinned back at them. She had one small burst of energy. It was the first since that horrible morning.

When the nice grey-haired lady came over to Penelope to take her bowl, Penelope weakly took hold of her hand. She looked up at the lady and pointed back to herself.

"Penelope," she said as she held the point to herself. She then pointed back to the nice lady and tilted her head as if asking a question. She was getting the hang of body language.

The lady smiled back at Penelope as if to say "finally you are talking." Using that same soothing voice that Penelope had grown to love she said "Nalehileehque."

Penelope worked hard to make her tongue work. "Na-le-hi-leehque."

The surrogate mother nodded and took the bowl. Penelope remembered that these were the people that Captain Jacobson had called "savages." However, that was not the way she was beginning to think of them. She had been totally dependent on these people for several days and they had been nothing but kind to her. How could they be more savage than the ones who left her vulnerable on the beach, alone with a sick husband?

In the morning Penelope was better able to stand alone. Her strength was still a long way off, but she was at least improving. Stepping out of the wooden hut that Owehela allowed her to share with his family, she could see that she was in a village with houses similar to his. In the middle of the community was a big house that was oblong. It did not look inhabited, but rather more like a meeting place for the others.

The next few months passed quickly. She traded languages with Owehela, each learning from the other a new language.

CHAPTER 4

Nalehileehque often practiced with them and learned quickly. They had become more proficient in the English language and were becoming more and more comfortable speaking that tongue. Penelope, likewise, was learning to love theirs. Eventually she was able to go back and forth between this new language and English.

Nalehileehque became more of a mother than anything she had ever known. Of course she had had nannies, Sunday school teachers, and other women in her life back in Amsterdam. But, none compared to her precious Nalehileehque. This wise woman had been patient and kind, yet firm and expecting, with her. She had not let Penelope feel sorry for herself, but instead had made her get up and work as much as she could with the other women. She had taught her how to prepare the delicious foods that the family grew in their fields. Penelope, in turn, had earned the respect of Owahela's household by not letting her wounds stop her from trying to do everything that everyone else did. They eventually saw past her wounds to the woman that even Penelope herself had not fully known until now.

She learned that Owehela and Nalehileehque were married. They had several children, all boys, including Tateuscung, the young man who had been in the woods that fateful day. Although he was not yet as wise as his father, he had a similar compassion for others and a genuine love for his family. He was the obvious pride of his parents and was gaining in respect from the rest of the village as he grew older.

Over the months, Penelope began to learn of their customs. They explained to her that they were Lenape. They had a genuine love of their families, just like the Dutch. They practiced a form of worship, sang songs, told stories, taught their children, cared for their elderly, and played games…just like the Dutch people did. She came to care deeply for these strange people. She missed her old life in a way, but also came to cherish the new customs she was adopting.

One afternoon a few months later Nalehileehque told Penelope that they had to prepare a big meal. The village was buzzing and the women especially were busy preparing more food than Penelope could remember in a while. She thought at first that it was to celebrate the return of a hunting party. But, they had had hunting party return celebrations before and it was nothing like this.

That evening the entire village gathered at the big house for a celebration. There were new people there that Penelope had not seen before, people from other villages. The men went to the sweat house to purify themselves before coming out to celebrate. They always did this before important events, but this one felt different. It was bigger and more solemn.

Owehela wore his Eagle feather and looked very regal. The women had colored their faces with red ochre and the men had taken special care to make their hair stand straight up in the middle. Everyone was decorated in their copper jewelry. Obviously, there was a special celebration going on, unlike any Penelope had seen.

All that evening, Penelope served the others along with Nalehileehque's nieces, Saagochque and Ayamanugh, the two young women who had helped her at Owehela's hut when she first arrived in the village. The women had not become friends, but had learned to tolerate each other. Saagaochque and Ayamanugh were jealous of the affections that Nalehileehque had shown Penelope. Since Nalehileehque had not had any daughters, these two women had served as substitute daughters for her all their lives and had no desire to share her affections with anyone else, least of all a white woman. They felt that they had been replaced in affection by Penelope, whom Nalehileehque had adopted. Their jealousy mounted even more when Penelope began wearing the beautiful and brightly colored head coverings Nalehileehque had made to cover her scars. No one else in the village had as beautifully woven adornments as Nalehileehque had made for Penelope.

Penelope listened to parts of the discussion the men were having and watched when they brought a dark-skinned man to the area outside the big house and tied him to a stake. He was not with this tribe and remained silent, head held up. He had been beaten, but his eyes were still full of pride and hate.

Penelope asked Saagochque if she should take the man some food.

CHAPTER 4

"Why?" asked Saagochque with a smirk. "He won't be alive much longer."

"What do you mean?" asked Penelope.

"That creature is a Mohawk. Some of our men captured him while on the hunting trip. The Mohawks are our enemy. He will be killed so there is no need to feed him tonight."

"But, why didn't they kill him instead of capturing him?"

"They brought him back here for the ceremony. He will be killed, skinned, and cooked. Our warriors will eat his body and gain his strength to help them fight against the other Mohawks."

Penelope could not believe what she was hearing. This was a truly savage act and could not believe that these kind people could do such a terrible thing. She would find out for herself from someone else. Saagochque was just trying to trick her. There was no way that Owehela would allow something like this to happen.

As Penelope continued to wait on the men in the big house she overheard them talking about the events to come later that evening. There was indeed to be a ceremony to transfer the strength of this prisoner to the men of the tribe. Her heart sank and she felt as though she would vomit. It was the first time she had seen the savage side of this village. She could not believe that the Lenape people who were so merciful could think that something so cruel should be celebrated.

Penelope could not stay. She could not bear witness to the events that were coming. She looked at the prisoner once again tied to the stake. He knew his fate and seemed to accept it with dignity. Even with all his bruises and contusions he held his head up and looked people in the eyes that dared to come close to him.

She had known how brutal the Mohawks could be. There was even a good chance that the two men who attacked her and killed Kent were Mohawks. She hated the two that killed her husband and left her for dead, but she still could not bear to see this type thing done to another human being, no matter how much revenge she wanted. She knew that she would not be able to stop this terrible event and to protest would mean almost certain death for her. It was unstoppable and each side knew what was about to happen, but she could not watch it either.

Penelope immediately left and walked to the stream that was close to the village. She could not let herself think about what was going to happen tonight. It was too much. It was like reliving the attack again. How could people be so cruel to each other? How could such kind people turn into such barbarians? What made people do that to each other?

Penelope stayed at the water all night. She could hear the chanting and hollering from the distance. It disgusted her and she longed to be back home in Amsterdam with her father. He was a demanding man, but right now she would take that. Crying in despair she fell on her face and prayed. Tonight, for the first time, she felt like God really heard her. It was the beginning of her new relationship with Him.

Chapter 5

Richard Stout, the man

Richard Stout looked over the side of the sloop to the ones following. The thirty-nine year old, an obvious leader, was ever vigilant in watching for signs of hostile natives. His broad shoulders and extraordinary build made him easily distinguishable from the rest of the settlers. His hair was red, unlike the rest of the men who still had hair as they had become prematurely grey. Although his skin was as pale as the others it seemed to have an unusual glow to it. Perhaps it was the fact that he was again on the water, or maybe it was the new adventure that lay ahead that caused him to shine. Either way, Richard stood out in the crowd of settlers.

He was going home, his new home. He watched the banks of the river for signs of anything that looked suspicious as the boat glided easily downstream. This new start would be just what he had been looking for all his life. He could make his own fortune, follow his own will, and live as he pleased. There would be no one to answer to except God. Finally, he was establishing himself, making a name.

His release from the Royal Navy four years earlier had been quite opportunistic for him in that he received his discharge papers in the

AS GOOD AS DEAD

New World. After his arrival in New Amsterdam he inquired of the Dutch about needing trained military men. Fortunately, the Dutch could use a fine burly man such as himself. No one questioned his ability to read or write. They just needed men who were willing to bear arms for the government. He got more than he bargained for with the Indian uprisings during this time. Adventure, however, had always been a friend of his.

Richard had seen more blood in the last two years than he had ever seen. The betrayal was prominent on both the white man's side and the Indian's side. Revenge begat revenge. Maybe the betrayal began with a lack of communication or maybe it began with greed. Either way, the battle for territory was raging and everyone was losing. It was getting harder and harder to keep things black and white on these issues.

The Lenape were still stinging from betrayals Director General William Kieft had ordered earlier in the year. The favoritism he showed towards the Mohawks had caused the River tribes to become increasingly angry towards the Dutch and the uprisings had even garnished a name, "Kieft's war." His foolhardy decision to massacre every living Lenape that was seeking shelter from the Mohawks at a Dutch camp had caused the remaining Lenapes outside the camp to band with other tribes, even though some of the tribes had always been enemies. But, a common enemy and a need to survive are stronger than years of hatred against each other. *Wars seem to make strange bedfellows,* Richard thought to himself.

Richard had seen the carnage first hand on one of the days after the massacre. That was when he decided that he had had enough of being in the Dutch military. He remembered vividly the images of soldiers flippantly playing kickball with the severed heads of the Indian children. It was the only time that Richard had ever vomited upon sight of the remnants of war. The dead, even enemy dead should have been shown more respect. He understood why the savages were angry. Sometimes he even wondered which side was actually savage. How could one enjoy the mutilation of the enemy's body in such a way? Even war should have some kind of honor. He

CHAPTER 5

turned in his resignation that very day, not being able to justify the fighting anymore.

It was soon after his resignation that he met Lady Moody in New Amsterdam. She needed patroons for a new settlement she was starting. He needed a fresh start, something to take him away from the images left in his mind from war. She was seeking religious freedom, he individual freedom, perhaps even from his own memories. Again, life had been fortuitous. It had placed him in the right place at the right time.

William Kieft was so inept at negotiating with the natives and even with his own people that many in New Amsterdam, including some of his own advisors, had signed a petition for his removal of office of Director General. It was directly because of his administration's corruption and his war that there were so many who did not want to start new settlements. Another door opened for Richard. Kieft was so desperate for settlers that he let a woman, Lady Deborah Moody, negotiate for a new settlement charter at Gravesend. He even granted her religious freedom instead of requiring that they have a Dutch Reform church there. These unheard of events, a settlement started by a woman and religious freedom, would never have come about if Director General Kieft had not been trying to save his own political hide.

Lady Moody had agreed to let Richard participate in the new settlement before their departure from New Amsterdam. He could begin his new life with new property and new opportunities. He just loved starting new things and the uncertainty of success, the very things to which his father had been so opposed. He relished in being different and embracing things that others found taboo. Even this notion of following a woman into a new settlement was unique. Who would have thought that a woman could design, recruit, and establish a new settlement? This most unique woman with an uncanny ability to negotiate successfully had a crazy idea of religious freedom and had even gotten the director general to agree to it. What would his father have thought about Lady Moody, and Richard's decision to cast lots with her?

AS GOOD AS DEAD

Richard thought about his father for a moment. He often did that. His father had been the very reason he had left his home town of Nottinghamshire, England. The demands of that man had been too great and the reward too little. Old John Stout was a part of the elite class there. He wanted Richard to be a part, too, but Richard had other ideas, other ways of thinking, and stubbornness kept both father and son from agreeing on much of anything.

"Richard, my boy, remember your status. You have responsibility to your family and to your station in life. You must keep your duty in mind in all decisions life requires you make." Richard's father's words were seared into his memory.

John Stout was a good man. He did manage to teach respect, loyalty, and honor to Richard. Mostly, though, his mother, Elizabeth Bee, had gently emphasized those traits. It was through her that most of the compromising was made by the two men. She seemed to be the only person to whom either man listened. Her gentle nature coaxed rather than preached and it was an approach that endured her to both of them.

For a moment Richard felt his mother's hand on his cheek and he closed his eyes, remembering her words. "Richard, I want you to be happy. Your father loves you very much, as do I. He wants what is best for you and that is why he demands so much." Ever the mediator, Elizabeth's words were not so much heard as felt. She had a way of calming them both.

The Stouts were descendents of royal Danish blood. Appearances were everything to the family, especially John. Richard had been reminded of who he was everyday of his life. His father had tried to force an education upon the young son. But, Richard would have no part of it. Adventure called to him. Reading and writing did not. Even Elizabeth's influence would not make him slow down to learn these things.

Richard hated pretenses, so the system that showed such utter contempt for those outside one's class never set well with him. His father had been consumed by it. He had always instructed Richard to marry the "right sort" of woman.

CHAPTER 5

"Marry for wealth and property, and if love is part of it, then you are truly a lucky man" John Stout's words burned. "Only the weak marry for love first. In marriage it is a secondary benefit."

Richard never really got over the look of disappointment in old John's eyes when Richard told him of his intentions to marry Amanda Petty, a bar maid. The memory hurt even until this day.

"Father, I love her" Richard said to a livid John that fateful night in the parlor of their home.

"What do you know of love? You are young, love will come many times! I know what you can offer her, but what can she bring to this marriage?" John tried to reason.

"She only need bring herself. I love her, not what she can bring to me."

"We have traditions, requirements...DUTY!" John had tried to make his son understand the importance of these things all his life and still the impetuous young man did not understand. "How can I make you see the magnitude of your actions if you go ahead and marry this woman? Can't you see that she is using you, making a mockery of you and your family?!"

"Amanda would never do that. She loves me and I love her!" Richard replied, anger building. "Status and money have nothing to do with it."

"I have raised a fool!" the old man said as he turned to a sympathetic looking Elizabeth.

The tension was so that Elizabeth felt she should intercede. Softly she tried to speak reason to her passionate son. "Richard, must you rush into this? Can't you slow down a bit? Think this through before you make a decision now that will affect the rest of your life. If Amanda truly loves you, she will wait and see if this is truly what the both of you want."

"Oh, we know what she wants all right," John's words were sharp. "She wants his money and to ruin this family!"

"That's not true! She loves me. Can't you understand that? And I love her! She would never do anything to hurt my family or me."

"Love? Love? She loves your money! What kind of dowry does

she have? What can she offer besides the experience of serving drinks and singing in a bar?"

"John! Can't you be a little more sensitive?" Elizabeth spoke unusually sharp to her husband. It was rare that she ever did this, so rare that both men stopped and looked at her for a moment, not sure of how to proceed with the argument.

Sarcastically and slowly, John looked at Richard and said "What, exactly, does young Amanda bring to the union? Marriage is a contract, a legal contract. Each party is to offer something in return for the other's promise of marriage. It is a lopsided contract if only one side has something to offer. I thought I had explained this to you."

"Amanda need only offer herself. That is enough for me."

"Yes, but it is not enough for the marriage contract. If you want to take her as a mistress, go ahead. I have no problem with your taking her as a mistress and having fun. To marry, however, is quite another thing!" John was getting crude.

"I will not impugn her honor by making her a mistress. She will be an honorable WIFE." Richard shot back. "She will not be made a whore!"

John looked incredulous. "Made a whore?" The old man turned and put his face directly into Richard's. "My son, she is already a whore! If you continue with your plans to marry this woman, I will have no choice but to banish you from my household. You will never be allowed to return to my house. Your inheritance, your stature, everything will be left here tonight. You will never again be welcomed here as long as I live. It will be to me as if you were never born!"

"John!" Elizabeth exclaimed in a hushed and horrified voice. She felt as though they had both punched her in the stomach.

"He is the one who is making this decision, Elizabeth, not I. If he wants to slum, he'll not bring the rest of the family down there, too."

Richard looked at his father, hurt at the words flung from his mouth. He looked at his shocked mother who could not keep the argument from going too far tonight. He picked up his hat, kissed his

CHAPTER 5

mother, and left the house forever, slamming the door as he went.

Richard rode his horse hard and fast to the inn. He saw Amanda as he burst through the door. Upon seeing him, she set down the drinks she was carrying and ran into his arms. He whisked her outside where they could talk privately.

"Richard, what's wrong? You look terrible!" She hugged him tightly as she spoke and he hugged back, grateful for her arms to be around him. Her petite body fit so snuggly in his embrace. He loved the way she fit in his arms.

"I'm all right." He pushed her a little back from him so that he could see her face and stared into her eyes. He had to bend down as she was ever so much shorter than he. Excitedly he asked "Amanda, do you still want to marry me?"

She looked at him adoringly. "You know I do. I cannot wait to be Mrs. Richard Stout!"

"Let's go then, tonight. Let's find a justice of the peace and get married tonight."

Amanda was suspicious because this was hasty, even for Richard. Something was wrong. "Why do you want to marry tonight? Can't we wait a few days and invite our friends and your family?"

"No. My father is determined to stop this marriage. We must get married as soon as possible." Richard was beginning to get a sinking feeling that his determination to get married out of love was now becoming a determination to undermine his father. He felt a gnawing in his stomach which was anything but a feeling of love.

"What do you mean? I know that your father did not like me, but why must we marry tonight? Why can't we have a big wedding? Your father will grow to like me eventually."

"Amanda, my father and I had an argument about our engagement tonight. He disowned me. I have nothing, no money, not even a place to sleep. But, we can live here in your room at the inn until I can find employment. You are working and it won't be long before I can work. I know I can have a job by the end of the week. We can make it. In a few years we can have our own place, make our own way. Everything will be all right, you'll see."

She pulled away from him and turned around and began to bite her fingernail. "Richard, are you saying that you are broke? You are poorer than I am? We won't be living at your father's estate? Is that what you are telling me?"

"Yes, but we won't be poor for long. I am strong and I have a good head on my shoulders. We will have a place of our own in no time at all."

"I will be staying right here, in this place that I hate, only now with you as my husband? How can you ask this of me? I thought we would be living at your father's estate with servants and class and money. I thought I would be leaving this place."

Richard stopped and looked at her. For the first time he was really seeing Amanda and it hurt. His naivety had never been as apparent to him as it was at this moment. His father had been right. Amanda did not want him, she wanted only what he brought to the bargaining table. She had used him as a fool to get out of her station in life, never mind love. She was no better than the upper class women he had dated, filled with ambition and lust for status. Appalled at the very site of her, the beauty he once saw was now as hideous as any nightmare he had ever had.

What was surprising to him was that he did not know which hurt worse, Amanda's betrayal or that his father had been right. He could not stand one more "I told you so" and it would most assuredly come. If he went back to his father's house tonight he would be giving in to defeat and be forced to live the life his father chose for him.

"Amanda, I thought you loved me."

"I do. But, Richard, I could marry any man who was poor. You were special because you were *not* poor."

There, it had been said. The words were said with a sickening sweetness that turned his stomach. He looked at her again, this time with repulsion. How could he have been so wrong? After a long pause, he turned away from her and grabbed his horse's reins. He never looked back, even as her apologies filled the air.

CHAPTER 5

He rode to the docks. He walked up and down the pier all night thinking about the fool he was. He stared out into the endless sea and longed for something, anything to take him away from this place. The humiliation was too great. He needed to be busy to keep his mind from thinking, from remembering. As the sun rose, he knew what he wanted to do. He went to the recruiting office and joined the navy. He never saw his father again, nor did he send word to him as to what happened.

The seven years he spent in the Navy had brought him more adventure than he had ever seen on land. Strangely, it brought him stability and discipline. It prepared him for the last few years he had spent in New Amsterdam. Finally, he had learned something that his father had tried to teach, but could not. The restlessness of his youth, however, was not quenched by the sea. It only fueled his passion for more adventure and he was finding plenty of this in the New World. It was just the place for him.

Richard looked over his shoulder at the boats behind, bringing his thoughts back to the present. Soon they would arrive at the landing at the home of Cornelis Hooglandt, the ferryman, and then they would be on to their new lives at Gravesend. Their new settlement was waiting for them, calling to them, expecting them. He could feel the impatience of the land desiring of trees to be felled, crops to be planted, and homes to be built.

Thomas Applegate approached Richard as he was thinking. He was an annoying little man, but Richard liked him somehow. Applegate did not have many people who tolerated him, let alone befriended him. Thomas had been Richard's lawyer on occasion and had helped him with the reading part of negotiating land sales. He talked too much for Stout. Richard had always believed that a man's words should count for something. Thomas believed that words were just words and not much else. But, Applegate was a loyal friend and businessman and Richard valued that loyalty.

"Not much longer now, eh Stout?"

"No. I suppose not. We have been fortunate thus far. I have not seen any sign of hostility."

"Well, we will get there, all right. No problems now," Thomas said as he slapped Richard hard on the back and gave a grin.

Richard looked at the silly little man for a second. It had not been that long ago that he would have lost his temper over a man putting his hands on him like that. But, time had taken away much of the temper and war had made him less ambitious for a fight. Richard took it for what it was, a simple hard pat from someone lacking the social graces of the elite class. When he thought for a second about his disdain for the elite class, it rather made him appreciate the pat. He gave Thomas an amusing smile and Thomas nervously smiled back.

Thomas had been a jack of all trades. He had owned a ferry service himself a few years ago, but it had ended in disaster. He had loaded his boat too heavy back in New Amsterdam and capsized his ferry. It caused five people and three horses to drown. The court had ordered Thomas to pay restitution, fines and for his boat to be staved. Yet, somehow he had managed to talk his way into getting his boat back. That man could talk, and upon occasion, talk well. Most of the time, however, his talk got him into trouble, not out of it.

Thomas Applegate was another "free-thinker" in the group. "Gossip" was the term most likely used by those who knew him longest. Not yet a patroon, he was merely along to inspect what the others were doing in case he wanted to join later. In the Bay Colony back in Massachusetts he had been a lawyer and even dabbled in weaving every now and then. But, he had gotten himself in trouble several times because of his speaking out of turn. Salem was not a tolerant town, nor did it care for free thinkers. The punishments were harsh for those who had their own ideas, let alone spoke them. He and his wife Eliza had paid many fines for slander over the years.

But, the final straw came when Eliza's last conviction of "swearing, reviling and railing" caused her to have to stand out on the public square for two days in stocks with her tongue in a cleft stick. They had packed up and moved to Rhode Island after that episode. They later joined their old friend Lady Moody in New Amsterdam

CHAPTER 5

when they purchased land there. Their new hope, their new start, could be in Gravesend, same as Richard's. Thomas vowed that things would be different here if he went ahead and decided to join the group.

Lady Moody had befriended Thomas when they both lived in England. He amused her. The young widow had set sail for the New World years ago after she had refused to baptize her infant son. Thomas the cavalier and his family went along. In the Bay Colony, Lady Moody had made enemies of the not-so-tolerant Puritans and was expelled from the settlement for her outspoken views on religion. None of the preachers there tolerated her, nor she them. In fact, one such preacher even went so far as to write other congregations about her. "She is a dangerous woman," he wrote.

She had mistakenly believed that the New World was a safe haven for religious freedom. The Puritans, however, believed that everyone had religious freedom only if he practiced the Puritan religion. There was no room for any other. Lady Deborah Moody had found the Puritans to be even less tolerant than her native churches of England.

After her refusal to submit to the Puritanical way of thinking and her subsequent excommunication, she and some of her fellow Anabaptists moved to New Amsterdam. Religious freedom could not be found there, either. The Dutch Reformed Church was the institutional religion. Although Kieft had been more tolerant than his predecessors in matters of religion, on the whole, government forced religion in Dutch New Amsterdam was no different than the English. Gravesend, she had vowed, would be a haven for free thinkers who need room to think and breathe and worship.

Gravesend was a very good spot for a settlement. It was at the mouth of the Narrows with New Amsterdam on the East side and the Atlantic Ocean on the other. It very easily could become an important harbor city, barring no Indian disturbances to hinder the trade. Prosperity, happiness, and freedom were at their fingertips.

Lady Moody had sectioned off Gravesend on a map before leaving New Amsterdam. It had been divided into four blocks, each block being again divided into ten equal sections, making a total of forty sections. The entire town was to be enclosed by a palisade-fence of trees that were at least seven feet high, providing some protection against invasive forces.

She had planned on a church to be built on one of the four squares, a school on the second, a town hall on the third, and a town cemetery on the fourth. There would be a common pasture for livestock and the farms would radiate from the village in diverging lines. This would allow the settlers to travel to and from their farms within the defenses of the town. The layout was organized meticulously and it was genius.

Finally, the ferry docked at Hooglandt's landing. The first few settlers disembarked. Richard escorted Lady Moody off the ferry to the Hooglandt residence, where she waited with Mrs. Hooglandt while the men unloaded the cargo. They unloaded livestock, food supplies, and wagons, everything they would need for the new settlement. The tiny river journey had been uneventful. Now, if it would only stay that way on the remaining land leg of the journey. *So far, so good*, Richard thought to himself.

The settlers camped at the Hooglandt bower that night. Early the next morning everyone loaded their wagons and hitched their mules and horses for the short travel distance to Gravesend. There was already a trail, so there was not a lot of wilderness to cut through. They should be there and tucked in by nightfall, that is, if they had not been detected by hostiles.

Thirty-nine soon-to-be patroons and their families were anxious to get to their new settlements. How different it would be in Gravesend from New Amsterdam. Instead of 18 languages being spoken there would one, English. Instead of only one religion, there would be many. Even the Quakers were finding Lady Moody tolerant to their faith.

By six o'clock that evening the last wagon had arrived in town. The real work would begin in the morning. Lady Deborah's house and a few others had already been built. But, trees had to be felled for the start of other new houses and barns so everyone helped each

CHAPTER 5

other, no one gaining anything more than his neighbor. They would also be working together watching for signs of hostility from the Natives. Little did the new settlers know that they were also being watched.

Chapter 6

The Search

Months passed and the Gravesend settlement grew. Houses were going up all around. Thomas Applegate eventually decided to participate in the settlement and agreed to buy a tract of land not far from Lady Deborah's house. It would be a while longer before Kieft had the charter drawn up anyway, having to conduct his own survey and draw up papers. Then he had to send the papers back to the home office in Holland to have them finalized before the settlers could officially own the charter.

Richard Stout, after building his house and barn, had settled into the farmer's life that he very much enjoyed. He owned property in New Amsterdam, but Gravesend was where he was determined to succeed. He had three male black servants and two female. He hated the word slave, which is what they were. He liked them and considered them more than property. He treated them well, but also knew that freedom was the one desire of their hearts. In fact, at the behest of George his main field hand, he was allowing any of the servants who wanted freedom to work off the debt of his price. George's debt would be paid in full in just one more year. He had also

CHAPTER 6

noticed that George was beginning to favor one of the female servants, Anna. More than likely George would try to pay for her freedom after he secured his own. That was fine with Richard. A free friend was better than an indentured one.

His farm soon came to include cattle, corn, and tobacco. He was known in the community for not speaking very often, but being heard when he did. He became well propertied, but not yet married. He always thought it would be nice to be married, but after Amanda he never really trusted a woman enough to give his heart.

Several times in those months he traveled to New Amsterdam for supplies, check on his property, and possibly enjoy the company of his few friends there. This particular summer day he traveled to town and happened across his old friend Danel Jacobson. They had served in the Navy together years before and he was happy to see his old friend. They decided to have supper together at the pub and chat about old times, and recent ones.

After the two had finished their meals Jacobson began to drink heavily. Richard had never known his friend to drink much. He had always been sober, logical, and matter-of-fact. Their shared traits may have been the reason for their friendship but, tonight his friend was different. Obviously, his heart was troubled and he needed to talk. Stout could not help but wonder what could have made his friend become this way.

After the Captain was sufficiently drunk enough to loosen his tongue, a strange story began to unfold to the uninitiated Stout. The tale began with the time being about last year when Jacobson's ship had gone down at Sandy Hook. All the passengers and crew had been forced to the hostile shore. Stout listened as Jacobson told his story with uneasiness, almost looking as if he was writhing in pain with each word.

"Aye, I remember it like it was yesterday. I have never in my life seen anything like this one woman!" Jacobson said as he took another drink. "A stubborn, crazy woman if ever there was one. I am reminded of why women are bad luck on ships every time I think of her."

AS GOOD AS DEAD

"What do you mean? Did she cause the wreck?" asked Stout.

"No. But, she could have caused us all to be killed! Her husband was ill with the fever he caught while at sea and was nearly dead by the time we wrecked. We all worked to get everyone to shore and with the natives looking for blonde scalps, that was no easy feat! But, by goodness, we all made it to shore alive, even the nearly dead one!" Jacobson winked, slapped the table and leaned back in his chair.

"Well, go on." Stout urged him.

"First, she wouldn't go to shore with the rest of the women. Oh no. She wanted to stay with her husband, said she. So, I let her stay with him until we could get him to shore. We were watching all around for the natives, scared witless, trying to get everyone to safety as soon as possible, not knowing when we would loose our scalps!" Jacobson waved his arms around and pointed to his own head, getting drunker and drunker.

"I told her we couldn't carry him because it would slow the group down too much, and even some of the passengers told her he would die before nightfall anyway, but she still would not leave him. She called me a savage for not taking him with the rest of the group. I tried to explain that to slow down would kill us all, but she wouldn't hear any of it. She refused to leave him. Finally we had to leave them there on the shore. I promised to send a rescue party back for them, and I did, too!" He took another hard swallow.

"What happened? Did you find them?" Stout was intrigued by now.

Jacobson paused, closing his eyes hard as if to block out the image that had haunted him over the last few months. Richard thought about how his friend suddenly looked very old. He could not tell the story without the drink to give him courage to speak. Guilt had consumed him and was eating the poor man alive, much more than any cancer could.

"We found part of them. As soon as we got the women and children to the fort, we gathered a rescue party and went back to the beach to see if there was anything left to rescue." He paused for a long while before he spoke again. "All we found was the man's

CHAPTER 6

naked, nearly headless, bloated body, a few pieces of tattered clothing, and a few bloody blankets. There was no sign of the woman. There is no telling what happened to her or if there is even a body left to find. I tried to tell her. I tried, but she wouldn't listen to me," he said almost as if asking for absolution.

Stout sat there in silence as his friend poured out his agonizing tale. After a long pause he asked "Do you remember their names?"

"Baron and Baroness Van Princes. Penelope was her name."

Stout decided his friend had had enough for one night. He paid the bill and got the captain a room. He carried his much drunk friend up the stairs and put him to bed. Richard couldn't help but feel pity for everything he had heard, but he also felt intrigue as to what would cause a woman to be this loyal. Why were some people fatally loyal and some not at all?

Richard got himself a room, too. He couldn't leave his friend like this. He had to make sure he was all right. All night long he wondered about the story he had been told. Had anyone searched anymore? Could she have survived?

The next morning Richard knocked on Jacobson's door. The captain opened it looking very much hung over. He was oblivious to the fact that he had spilled his heart out last night, in fact, he couldn't remember most of the day before. At first glance Richard wondered if his friend felt as bad on the inside as he looked and reeked on the outside, but he had no time for pity this morning. He had a proposal.

"Jacobson, do you want to go find out what happened to this woman Penelope?" Richard began immediately, moving faster than bloodshot eyes could follow.

"What are you talking about?" Jacobson said as he held his aching head.

"You told me last night about a woman who wouldn't leave her sick husband on the beach. You found him, but you never found her. Do you want to try to find her now?"

"We looked for her. Days we looked for her, but we never found her." Jacobson said, not really wanting to pursue the matter further as it only added to his guilt and pain.

"Well, if you want to try again, I will go with you. You know where you left them and I know a few Indian words to trade with. Maybe we can find her." Stout was hopeful-sounding, and the voice was too optimistic for the ears of someone with a hang over.

"There's nothing left of her! Don't you understand? We found the mangled body of her husband. I won't even think about what they did to her before they killed her!" Jacobson lied. He had thought, and often, of what the savages may have done to her before they killed her.

"Did you ask the Indians about this white woman?" Stout logically asked.

"No. Why would I put myself in a predicament to ask savages about it? They would lie anyway." Jacobson's tone turned into mockery. "I can see it now. Oh, by the way Mr. Indian, do you have a white woman held captive in your village that you and your friends have repeatedly raped over the past year or so? Or, do you know where the body is of a white woman you killed on the beach? You do remember her husband, don't you? You left him naked and mangled there after you scalped him!" He waved his hands and rolled his eyes as he sat down on the bed and grabbed his boots.

"They are not all like that. Sometimes they'll trade for hostages. It could be that she's a hostage waiting to be ransomed. Would you be interested in investigating it?"

"Do you think if she's been in captivity for more than a year she has any sanity left? Do you think it would be worth risking our necks to see?" Jacobson argued.

"Yes. I think she has earned at least an attempt. How much is her kind of loyalty worth? How many friends, let alone women, would have stayed with you if it had been you that was sick? Have you ever had anyone sacrifice for you like that?" Stout replied.

Jacobson hung his head, wanting to be rid of the images in his tortured mind. Absolution could be his if he merely attempted to find this woman. He could truly give himself another chance for self forgiveness. Was Stout asking so much? Wouldn't her rescue help him as much as it would help this woman? *Why is Stout so*

CHAPTER 6

interested? he wondered through bloodshot eyes.

"Why are you doing this? Why do you want to go risking your neck for someone you don't know?" Jacobson was puzzled.

"Because, in all my years, in all my travels, I have never heard of someone with such loyalty or love for someone else. I want to see what one looks like with that much devotion." Richard said with all conviction. Then, turning impish he said "Besides, we haven't had a good adventure together in years. We're overdue."

Jacobson smiled back at his friend. That look and sound of hope was too much to pass up. He had to take the chance to get his life and sanity back. Finally, he nodded. "Well, let's get to it."

That afternoon the two men gathered supplies they would need for their search effort. They planned their strategy, talked about how to avoid Indian hostility, and Jacobson actually caught some of the enthusiasm his friend exuded. It was the first time in more than a year he was able to actively pursue something with optimism. He could actually set aside the heavy weight of guilt he had carried for so long because he was *doing* something, not just sitting back and replaying the images in his mind. His step was quicker and his heart had become lighter. It was amazing how Stout had actually given hope to him. But was hope unfaithful? Would it be taken away as quickly as his friend had offered it? Jacobson shook off that thought. He would find out, one way or another, what became of the woman, either way, he would know and the burden would be easier. It was all he could cling to at this moment.

Early the next morning the duo set out to find out what happened to this woman named Penelope. Danel led the way back to the place where they had left the couple last year, through the thick forest to the beach off Sandy Hook. By late afternoon they had reached their destination. Nothing was left now of any kind of skirmish or even evidence that people had once been there.

This was the starting point, however. "Where did your search party go from here?" asked Richard.

"We went along the beach, north and south," was the reply.

"Did you go inland, over there to the forest?" Richard inquired.

AS GOOD AS DEAD

"No. We thought that the beach held more promise. If there was any search inland by anyone, it was not very far."

"Let's try inland then since you have covered the beach already."

The two rode their horses into the wooded area east of the beach. There was nothing now to indicate any human sign of life, just an old hollow tree that neither man noticed very much. They rode past it deeper into the forest. The pace was slow and methodical, looking for any sign that might be helpful, each knowing the likelihood of that was near impossible.

Richard remembered Applegate telling him a while back about a trading post just to the South. Perhaps they could pick up some information there. After looking around the area and finding absolutely no clues the duo pointed their horses southwest towards where they hoped to find a trading post.

The area was still dangerous as the Indians were still hot from Kieft's skirmishes. The captain was not as familiar with land life as Richard had become, but his eyes were sharp by now. They watched for any sign of aggression, easing through the forest more so than merely riding. The natives could be anywhere in this area and they certainly knew the territory better than either of the white men.

After several miles they saw what looked like a crude settlement, not all white and not all native. It must be the post. They rode closer and closer feeling more at ease because the natives surrounding this area would more likely be concerned about trading fur and wampum than scalping heads. They would camp here tonight, ask questions, and set out again in the morning.

The camp consisted of a couple of log houses and a few stick round houses. There were several small fires around sending the smells of game cooking over them waffling through the evening air. Neither man had realized they had not eaten all day, being too intense on the search and watching for signs of hostiles.

They were greeted by a man named Benjamin McPherson, a big burly Scotsman who liked to drink, fight, and trade. He came out of the western most log house and hollered at Stout. Dressed in leather and bearded, he looked very much like the trapper that he was.

CHAPTER 6

"Stout, how're ye doing?" A smiling McPherson said in a thick Scottish accent as he grabbed Richard's hand, almost before Richard could let go of the horse. "I thought ye took up over at Gravesend. What brings ye way over here?" Then, looking at Jacobson, he said "And who have ye brought with ye?"

"Benjamin McPherson, allow me to introduce Captain Danel Jacobson." Stout said.

Immediately McPherson grabbed his hand, not so much in greeting, but to test the strength of the newcomer. Jacobson's handshake gave back as much as it got. Both men soon had the other's eyeballs nearly popping out, but neither tried to show the other how much it hurt. McPherson would be drunk by nightfall and would probably try to fight soon after. Jacobson might just be good sport.

"Pleased to meet you," McPherson said after sizing up the new guy.

"Pleasure's all mine," said Jacobson likewise, both men grinning through clenched teeth. Neither man wanted to be the first to release the handshake as it had now become a contest.

Richard had seen this ritual all too often and had made a point not to warn his friend. He always became amused whenever McPherson met a new man, especially one that might look like a good sparring partner. He was always on the verge of fighting, not in a mad sort of way, but in a sporting kind. McPherson would fight as hard as he could trying to beat his opponent, then get right up and buy the poor soul a drink right afterwards. It wasn't that he hated anybody; he just loved to drink and fight. He usually liked the men he fought and God help those he hated that fought him. Finally the two released the grip simultaneously, proving that each was as stubborn as the other.

"We need to camp here tonight if that is all right with you," said Richard. "We're looking for someone and hope we can get some information while we are here."

"Sure. Sure. Stay as long as ye want. There're not many people here this week like there was last. This place was covered. Ye should've seen it." He pulled his pipe out of his pocket and dipped it into his leather tobacco bag. He took a twig and with it reached over to one of the fires, lit it, and brought the fire back to his pipe.

After a few puffs to make sure his pipe was smoking, he continued. "We had a big trade last week. Indians came from all around to trade fur. They wanted whiskey, but of course, by law I could no' trade it with them." With this he winked at Stout. "I abide by the law, Stout. The law says no whiskey, so I don't trade whiskey. Besides, I'd rather keep that for myself."

Stout knew better. This man had never passed up money. "Of course, of course. I'm not here about the whiskey. You said there was a big trade last week. Did you hear anyone mention a white woman possibly living with Indians?"

McPherson nodded. "I have heard something like that. A white woman was found in the woods last year, pretty mangled up, left for dead. No one knew who she was, just that she was as close to death as anyone ever came and lived to tell about it, as good as dead she was."

Jacobson's heart began to race. No, he would not let hope blossom. He would keep a logical head about him. This may not be the same woman. After all, he said she was found in the woods, not on the beach.

"Where is this woman?" asked Jacobson.

McPherson puffed a few more times on his pipe, sizing up the competition. It had been a whole week since he last got to spar and he was overdue.

"I'll tell ye, but ye have to do something first."

Richard grinned. He knew what was coming. Jacobson had a puzzled look on his face as he stared at Richard. McPherson just stood there, grinning at Jacobson through the pipe and smoke.

"Who, me?" was Jacobson's reply. "What do you want me to do?"

"Well, it's been a whole week since these men around here got a chance to bet on a sport. Ye are about my size. I think we could take on a fight tonight and see how things go. If ye do that, I'll tell ye what I know."

CHAPTER 6

Jacobson had heard about these crazy traders, but had never really run across one so brazen.

"No. I didn't come here to fight with you. I came looking for a shipwrecked woman."

Richard pulled his friend to the side. "Danel. We need this information. You are going to have to fight this man." Inside Stout was vastly amused at the situation in which his friend found himself. "Don't worry. He gets drunk before every fight. Besides, if we give good sport, we might be more likely to get information."

By now Richard could hardly contain the grin. Jacobson could fight well, he just didn't like to. He preferred the logical way, the negotiating way. He had had his share of scrapes in the past, but he never went looking for a fight. The Scotsman never looked to negotiate anything; fists were his method of arbitration.

"Why should I agree to fight this madman? We are not even sure this is the right woman he speaks of." Jacobson protested.

"Yes, but we don't know she isn't either." Stout countered.

Jacobson thought how this must be part of his penitence, fighting with a crazy man. If this was part of the price, he would just have to pay.

"Oh, all right. But, YOU buy drinks afterwards."

Richard grinned. "Done."

They turned back to McPherson who was still standing there smoking his pipe. It had never taken him that long to make a decision on a fight. Sometimes he didn't decide at all, his fist just took a crazy turn into someone's face and the decision was made for everyone.

Richard said "Get your bets up McPherson. Jacobson agrees. But, you have to give us information on the woman afterwards."

"Aye. Done deal." He looked Jacobson up one side and down the other. Each circling like a couple of rams readying for the inevitable. "See you in two hours," he said and then went into the house.

Stout and Jacobson looked at each other. Then, they went to the other side of the trading post and made camp close to the Indian round houses. Since this was a trading area, they knew the Indians were more than likely not hostile. And, if they spoke any kind of

AS GOOD AS DEAD

English maybe they could tell them something of the woman.

It didn't take long for the news to get around the post that a big fight was the entertainment tonight, the newcomer against McPherson. Since every man that had remained in camp had had to fight him at one time or another they knew that tonight would be interesting.

The time came for the main event. McPherson, true to form, showed up half drunk, but still sober enough to know where to put his punches. Jacobson, the underdog, was a surprise to everyone except Richard and McPherson. Both of these men had known how to size up a fighter and they knew Jacobson would be able to hold his own.

Immediately after the shirts came off, the hollering began. Gathered in a circle, the men made a ring for the two fighters. McPherson threw the first punch landing it square in the jaw of Jacobson. He fell backwards against the crowd and was immediately thrown back to his opponent who was standing there smiling in a way a man with too few teeth would. The crazy Scotsman loved this and the fun had just started. Jacobson had been a little timid at first, but not now.

Face punches, left, right, and body punches were thrown by each man, landing with precision on their targets. The men betting on the event found out soon that Jacobson could give as good as he could get and was quite possibly the best sparring partner they had seen McPherson take on.

The fight lasted for more than an hour with a break about every 15 minutes or so to get a drink of water and spit out a tooth or two. McPherson didn't have many left to knock out. Neither man was willing to give up. The fight continued at full speed until finally both men were on their knees facing each other throwing one exhausted punch after another, looking as if taking turns.

At last, Jacobson took one deep breath and threw his final do-or-die punch which landed squarely on McPherson's already broken nose. That was it. The Scotsman fell backwards and the fight was over. After Jacobson saw that McPherson had collapsed, he let himself go and did likewise.

CHAPTER 6

Amidst cheers and jeers a couple of men in the crowd got buckets of water and doused the two fighters on the ground. Richard helped them both up. Both men's legs were shaky, but neither admitted to it. They shook hands as McPherson's swollen, bloody mouth tried to form a grin. Jacobson now had the old man's respect. Jacobson, for some reason, felt strangely better for having released some of his rage. He had had a purpose for the release which gave him some kind of justification for it.

"Let's go get a drink" said McPherson. "I haven't had a fight like that since I can't remember when. I did no' know the Dutch could fight so good."

"I didn't know Scotsmen could take a punch so good," said Jacobson with a grin.

The crowd dispersed with their winnings and losses, now having something to talk about for the next couple of days. There is nothing like a good fight to talk about while one passes the time at a trading post. Barring an interesting Indian uprising, the trading post was pretty tame most of the time.

Stout, Jacobson, and McPherson retired to McPherson's log cabin. His wife, a Lenape he called Agnes, had his drink poured for him when he sat down at the table. She had some cornbread, ham, and beans left on the table from supper. She had grown accustomed to his antics after living with him for some time.

"This is my wife, Agnes," McPherson said. He leaned forward in almost a whisper to the two men at his table, "I could no' pronounce her Indian name, so I call her Agnes. She don't mind and I like the name. She don't speak much English and I like a woman who don't say much."

Richard took the opportunity to continue his investigation. "Speaking of women and Indians, you said you would tell us what you know about the woman we were speaking of earlier."

"Aye. I did. Agnes comes from a village not far from here who has a white woman living with them. She came to them about a year ago. Poor woman, they said she was scalped and gutted and left for dead. Agnes' cousin found her and brought her back to her village, where they helped her heal."

"Can you or Agnes show us where she is? Can she be ransomed?" Richard asked. Jacobson wanted to ask the questions himself, but his mouth was swelled so badly it hurt to speak.

"Yeah. I can show you. As far as ransoming goes, we will just have to go ask. Her cousin's name is Owehela. He makes the decisions over there. I had to trade 3 horses and 10 beaver furs for Agnes when he brought her with him last year. He drives a pretty hard bargain." He nodded back to Agnes "I have no' been to their village. She came with Owehela when he came to trade last year. Come to think of it, last week I noticed he was speaking more English." McPherson attention turned back to the table and he saw that his buddies' glasses were still full. In mock anger he said "Now, turn up those glasses and get drunk. It hurts to be sober!"

Jacobson nodded in agreement and drank not only what was in his glass, but also what was left in the jug closest to him. Richard drank enough to pacify his old friend McPherson, but not enough to loose his wits. After all, he wasn't the one with the swelled face, Jacobson was.

Chapter 7

Gravesend settled

Lady Deborah kept a watchful eye on her new home of Gravesend. She had been the chief judge in a few of the matters of small disputes and had more than once saved Thomas Applegate from himself. However, his unbridled speech had still gotten him into trouble from time to time. Many of his afternoons were spent in stocks outside the widow Moody's house, usually after he had had too much to drink and his tongue broke loose. He had been thrown out of the new pub more times than anyone else in Gravesend. If he was not in the stocks in front of her house, he was either working on his farm away from the temptation to talk or back at his home in New Amsterdam.

She and several of the men of the settlement had negotiated with the local Indians for the re-purchase of the land they now settled. Although Kieft had purchased it from the Carnarsie, there were other tribes who felt that they also owned some part of it. Since the Dutch did not keep records as well as the English the Gravesend settlers had no choice but to appease the Indians who felt offended. Stout, Stillwell, Applegate, Walter Wall and the other men met with the local sachems and negotiated for the land. A little wampum and a few hogshead of tobacco later and the Indians would not dispute the settlement. At least the peaceful ones wouldn't anyway. By treating these tribes with respect, they had gained peace that had eluded some of the other settlements.

They had had a few scary days with different Indians in the months since they came there. Several of the River tribes had become increasingly hostile. There were so many tribes fighting amongst themselves that she was beginning to lose track of just who was whom. Then Kieft added to the trouble by keeping them stirred by his many massacres, continuing to mutilate the corpses of the Indian women and children. Fortunately for Moody and the others, these Indians had aimed their anger at the Dutch. The Gravesend settlers being English were spared some of the fighting. However, some of the tribes didn't know or didn't care about the difference. They just wanted to kill white men, any white men. It had gotten so bad at one point that Lady Moody began to doubt whether the settlement was even a good idea or not, especially after she learned of her friend Anne Hutchinson's death.

Hutchinson had been her friend back at the Bay Colony. She also had not believed in infant baptism and was a religious dissenter, just like Moody. Neither woman valued the importance of someone else's view of religion. They believed that salvation was through grace and not given out by man. They held the view that the individual, and not the church, was responsible for his own relationship with God. This idea was threatening to the male church leaders. These women actually held church meetings in their homes and their congregation was growing!

Neither woman, nor those that met with them, believed in the office of preacher. The church elders believed that it would not be long before their authority would be challenged by the remainder of the community if they allowed Anne to continue her dissent. They had to do something, so they began to rebuke the women and challenge them to repent of their usurping of authority over men.

The difference in the treatment of Hutchinson and Moody was

CHAPTER 7

that the Bay Colony Governor John Winthrop had seemed to like Moody and despise Hutchinson, referring to her as the "American Jezebel." Both women had been excommunicated from the Church of Salem after being repeatedly admonished by the church elders. Moody and her followers had left. Anne stayed.

"Anne, please come with me. You are not safe if you stay here" Lady Deborah pleaded to her friend."

"Deborah, I understand why you are leaving and it is right for you. You are my friend and I appreciate what you are saying. However, I must stay and make them understand that what they are doing is wrong. I have prayed about this and I know that what I am doing is right, even if it is difficult."

Lady Deborah looked at her friend and admired her courage and convictions. These church men that Anne argued with, however, would never change and they had the power to hurt, even destroy those that contradicted their teachings. Torture of those who disagreed with them was not uncommon. A looming feeling of doom held its tentacles around Deborah's heart as she continued to plead with Anne.

"You can write to them to explain your understandings. You do not have to stay here to fight them. Come with me and we'll find a better place, one with tolerance and love. Even the Bible tells us to shake the dust from our feet as we leave a place that does not accept truth.

"Yes, but if I don't explain that their thinking is hurtful, who will? Who will show them the love of God for all, regardless of standing, if not I?

"Anne, I know you mean well, but please…"

"Deborah, I love you. Go with God and pray for me and my family in these trying times."

Lady Deborah did pray and often. Anne went on to trial, a mock trial with all the church leaders who disagreed with her presiding. While she argued eloquently and even used the Bible to turn the leaders' own words back on them, she was still found guilty of antinomianism and was banished from the Colony. At the time, that punishment seemed less harsh than the rack or stoning.

Lady Moody and her followers settled at New Amsterdam before coming to Gravesend, but times had been harder for Anne. Winthrop banished Anne and all her family from the Colony and threatened prosecution to anyone who harbored or helped them. Such was Winthrop's hatred for Anne and her family that a friend of theirs, William Thorne was fined 6 2/3 pounds for concealing, hiding, and supplying Anne's son and son-in-law after the banishment. Winthrop didn't just want her gone; he wanted her on her own in a savage land without any sort of aid at all. He wanted her broken, humiliated, hurt, and begging for his mercy. Winthrop must have been disappointed because Anne never begged for his help, mercy, or forgiveness.

Anne's husband had become ill during all this turbulence. After his death her family settled at Pelham Bay. It was there that they were all, but her daughter Susanna, murdered by Indians. Winthrop did not mourn her tragic end.

Lady Moody would never get over the loss of her dear friend. In ways Anne's convictions cemented her own, but in others she doubted leading more people down this unsafe path. Yet she knew that the ones that came with her to Gravesend held the same freedoms dear that she did. She never understood why someone would want to dictate religion, a very personal thing, to someone else anyway.

Many of the settlers built their boweries in Gravesend while still holding onto their homes in New Amsterdam. They traveled back and forth between the two towns until Gravesend could be legally and officially obtained from the West India Company. Many of the men would not let their families come to Gravesend until they felt that the uprisings were somewhat settled. Then, after the legal matters were finalized their plans were to sell their properties in New Amsterdam for permanent residence in Gravesend. A few families,

CHAPTER 7

however, threw caution to the wind and just stayed at the new settlement.

Lady Deborah had not sold, but held on to her other properties, including the one in the Bay Colony. Winthrop may have driven her out physically, but she would retain her property there, even if only to annoy him. She was among those who were determined to stay in Gravesend with her family. Her only family was her young teenaged son.

Henry Moody, Deborah's son, was sixteen and nearly grown. Lady Moody had been careful to make sure that he was educated in a fine manner. She had acquired the finest library in all of the New World making sure that Henry had access to knowledge at his mere fingertips. She was very proud of the man he was becoming. She had made sure that he had been taught that it is possible to disagree with someone, but still think highly of them. Tolerance was a trait that she made sure she passed on to him and, even though they had been threatened by some natives, she taught Henry that not everyone who looked the same thought the same.

Henry was not particularly outgoing as a child. He was content to be by himself reading or hunting or in some other way busying himself. He knew his mother liked to talk and he liked to listen so it made for an easy relationship. Henry often hunted for deer and other game in the surrounding areas of the settlement by himself. While in the woods he began to meet friendly Indians that liked to trade. So, he began friendships with the natives and soon he was bringing a few of his friends home for supper. Lady Deborah didn't mind the extra plates set. She loved company and was interested in the natives, particularly because they were her son's friends and she was happy that he finally had someone to be friends with.

One evening Henry brought home an Indian he had been trading with over the past few weeks. They had hunted and fished together and had become fast friends. This night Henry had a rabbit skin to trade and his Indian friend had a new corn pipe. Henry had wanted a pipe but Lady Deborah had forbid it which made the trading even more appealing because what mother didn't know wouldn't hurt her.

He stopped to hide his new corn pipe under the front steps before entering the house.

"Mother, I brought someone home for supper," said Henry as he burst through the door more loudly than usual.

Lady Moody turned around to find her teenage son standing beside a very tall dark young man not much older than Henry with a strange haircut dressed in fringed leather and one feather sticking up out of the band that wrapped around his forehead. He had leather shoes on his feet and a tobacco purse around his neck. Henry's mother was getting used to this site and didn't react to the native standing in her kitchen.

"Hello. My name is Mrs. Moody," she said holding out her hand to greet the stranger.

"Hello. I am Tateuscung" said the obviously articulate native returning the white woman's greeting in like manner.

"Sit down. I have turkey and beans tonight. Henry killed it yesterday when he went hunting."

"Thank you." Tateuscung said while sitting self-consciously down at the table.

Lady Deborah sat down with the two young men and fixed their plates for them. She talked of her day and asked about theirs. Tateuscung and Henry did not talk unless asked a question. That didn't matter because Lady Moody had enough conversation to keep things going for quite a while. She always did.

Lady Deborah was also good at discernment. While it looked to everyone else like she talked and did not notice others, she was all the while sizing up her guest as she felt all good mothers should do. She got the feeling that she would probably like Tateuscung very much. He knew English better than any native she had met, appearing to be at ease in the language although a little uneasy with white mannerisms

"Where are your people?" asked Lady Deborah a while into the meal.

"We live across the bay" was the answer.

"What do your people call themselves?" She knew that all the

CHAPTER 7

tribes referred to themselves in a different way.

"Lenape" was the only reply.

She was trying to initiate more conversation from the quiet young man, but he did not elaborate. She continued with her questioning. "You speak English very well. Do your people speak English?"

"Some of us do. I have a teacher who has helped me. She lives in my father's house in my village. She has taught my family to speak English."

"You have a white woman living in your village?" Now Lady Moody was very curious.

"Yes. She has been with us for a while." Tateuscung did not appear to be comfortable with this turn of the conversation.

"How did this woman come to live at your village? What is her name?" Lady Moody ignored the young man's uneasiness.

Tateuscung turned to his new friend Henry and said "thank you for the meal. I must go now."

Henry understood his friend's reluctance to be interviewed. His mother could be quite persistent when she wanted. "I'll walk with you to your canoe" he said as they both got up from the table.

Tateuscung thanked Lady Moody for the meal. Penelope had told him how much a word of thanks meant to white people, especially the women. Although he did not understand why the white people liked so many words he tried to be courteous.

On the way to the canoe Henry tried to apologize to his new friend for the inquisition his mother had just given him. Tateuscung stopped his young friend before too many words were spoken. "No need to apologize. Your mother is very nice woman. She likes to know about things."

Henry smiled. "Yes, she does. She tries to find out about everything that's going on around her."

"She is good woman. I will see you soon."

Tateuscung shoved off from the shore and moved quietly in the moonlight across the bay. The evening air was cool but comfortable and unusually warm for this time of year. Henry turned around and headed back to his mother's house.

"He seemed like a very nice young man. How long have you known him?" asked Lady Deborah as Henry came in through the door. She had already washed the dishes and put her things away for the evening.

"Oh just a little while. We hunt and fish together sometimes. I met him one day while I was fishing, didn't even hear him come up. All of a sudden he was just standing there beside me telling me I could catch more if I moved a few hundred feet down. When I saw the string of fish he had I did what he said. He just seems to show up sometime."

"His English is very good. Do you know anything about his teacher?" Deborah was picking Henry for information now and he knew it.

"I never asked and he never told. I am going to bed now. Good night mother." With that Henry went into his bedroom and closed the door. No more information tonight.

Lady Deborah was intrigued by Tateuscung's teacher. She had done a good job teaching English, but what would a white woman be doing with a village of Indians? Was she there willingly or was she captive? These thoughts bothered her all night.

The next morning Lady Deborah went to the beach to dig for clams. She liked doing that because she could get away from all the others in the settlement. It was so warm that morning she tied her skirt up above her knees and walked barefoot on the sand. Baring all that skin was a daring thing to do, but she was alone and no one could see. She could let herself go and just enjoy the sunshine. *Imagine what old Winthrop would have said and done if he had seen me show my legs!* She thought in amusement.

After gathering nearly a bucket full of clams she began to feel that something was not right. It was an eerie feeling that was hard to describe. She saw no one, but could feel the weight of a stare as she strolled along. It was a dangerous and uneasy feeling. She let her dress back down, picked up her bucket and walked hurriedly back to her home.

When she got back to her house she went to the kitchen to give her

CHAPTER 7

servant Frieda the clams she had foraged on the beach. To her surprise there was last night's guest sitting at the table with Henry. He stood when she entered the room.

"Hello, Tateuscung. What brings you back so soon?" It was the only thing she could think to say since she was still unnerved by the feeling she had gotten on the beach.

"Henry is my friend. I came back to warn you that there is an attack on your village planned by some of the tribes who have banned together."

"What have you heard?" she asked causing the mood in the room to instantly become graver.

"Some of the river tribes are banding together to destroy the white villages. They attacked a white village last night and they plan to be here tonight. I did not know about it until this morning when I saw scalps they took. I was in a tree when some passed by. I heard them talking about what they had done. When I found out about the plans to come here I wanted to warn my friends. I want you to know…my people are not among these." Tateuscung said.

Lady Moody realized that she had sized up her son's new friend correctly. He was someone she could trust. She was thankful for her son's meeting with this young man.

"I must let the others know so we can do something. I know that you risked your life by telling us this news. I cannot thank you enough for all you have just done."

"Stay alive. It will be thanks enough," said Tateuscung. "I must go now."

Tateuscung left and was soon out of site. Lady Deborah and Henry were left with what to do with the news. They decided that since Mr. Stout was out of town they would tell Nicholas Stillwell. He was a good leader and would know what to do. Lady Deborah went to tell him the news, leaving Henry to help Frieda and the other servants secure their home.

Nicholas Stillwell listened carefully as Lady Deborah replayed the conversation she had with her Indian friend this morning and what she had sensed on the beach. He knew that Lady Moody was not a woman easily rattled so he gathered a few men, James Hubbard, George Baxter, Thomas Spicer, and Walter Wall to take a look around. The fence surrounding the settlement was not finished yet so there were several places someone who wanted to do harm could get in.

The men took a look around in a way as not to look like they were scouting. They split up and decided to meet back at Stillwell's house. They had all been in the military at one time or another in some capacity so they were experienced in watching for hostilities.

A couple of hours later the men and Lady Deborah met back at Stillwell's house as agreed. Every man had seen some kind of Indian movement. Stillwell had seen several Indian men in canoes, an unusual thing to see so many at one time without a special trade or meeting going on. Wall had seen the same thing from his vantage point. Hubbard, Baxter, and Spicer had each seen from one to four Indians each in the woods in their different locations, also unusual. Something was definitely going on. Each white man had been covert in their scouting by looking like they were doing some sort of daily duty, not bringing attention to themselves or calling out.

"The Indians I saw looked like Raritan. They did not look like the same tribes that are our immediate neighbors," said Hubbard.

This caused Lady Deborah's blood to go cold and a shiver ran up her spine. Her friend Anne had been killed by that tribe. They were not ones to be trifled with.

"Why would they want to come here?" asked Lady Deborah.

Baxter spoke up. He had heard of the latest Kieft massacre a few weeks ago. "They are still warring with Kieft. His brutality at Corlaer's Hook and at Hoboken caused all this fighting we have had in the last few months. David de Vries told me the whole story. He said that the River Indians had sought shelter from the Mohawks with the Dutch at those places, much like they have done in the past. De Vries wanted to take that opportunity to secure a treaty for peace with them seeing that it was a good time to do so, but Kieft would not hear of it. He and a few of his cronies decided to order a surprise attack while the Indians slept. Their military colored the ground and the

CHAPTER 7

river crimson with the blood they let from the natives that night. DeVries said he saw the butchery by the light of the burning wigwams from the ramparts of Fort Amsterdam while Kieft cowered down in the protection of those walls, not being man enough to be at the sites to see his handiwork firsthand."

Stillwell spoke "Kieft gave no thought to the gravity of his order? I can believe that."

"De Vries said the massacres, and that is what they were—massacres—were horrible that night. He said that the soldiers threw the children into the water and when their parents went in to save them the soldiers drove them all back into the water to be drowned. Others were killed while they slept or ran. They spared no one," Baxter continued.

"It looks like the remnants regrouped to get revenge. The few fights we have had since we have been here have been bad, but it looks today like they are planning to do to us what Kieft had done to them," said Hubbard.

"We have to get everyone out of here, but we don't need to go to New Amsterdam where Kieft is right now. Should we go to Fort Amersfoort?" Lady Deborah broke in.

"I think it would be a good idea," said Stillwell. "We can get the women and children there immediately."

"If there is that much movement now, there will be no way we can get out of here undetected." was her reply.

"You may be right," said Hubbard. "If they see the women and children leaving they may go ahead and attack. If we stay here and thwart their surprise tonight we may be able to stay them off. After all, we have guns and they don't."

Baxter broke in "we don't THINK they have guns. We don't know what they have been able to steal or trade for."

"Exactly" said Wall. "If we stay here and batten down, we might have a chance—all of us, but if we make movements that alerts them to the fact that we know of their plan it will doom many of us."

They all decided to meet the night time surprise with a night time surprise of their own. They decided to immediately clear the overgrown brush to take away some of the hiding spots. The men worked in a fury to clean as much as they could.

Next, Stillwell divided the men into two groups. They lay in wait for nightfall at Lady Deborah's house, armed and alert. Henry participated with the men in his home. His mother had wanted him to learn of tolerance and negotiation, but she knew that there were times when a man had to fight. This was one of those times. As much as she wanted it to be easy, she knew that life could not always be that way.

The fighting began immediately after nightfall. There was a great cry from the woods and before long Gravesend's quiet evening was severely disturbed. The Indians had thought the residents were asleep. They were wrong.

Stillwell had the first group fire into the attacking savages and many were immediately killed. After the initial round the first group fell back to reload while the second group took their places and fired round two killing many more of the attackers. The first group, now reloaded, came back up to take their turn again only to see that the Indians were retreating.

They had expected sleeping victims but found armed defenders. The Indians were ill prepared that night to fight that type of battle. They would not try another attack again until they were better prepared. Gravesend had won this battle tonight, but things there would never again be the same.

Chapter 8

Rescued

Penelope blocked out the events of the festival from last month. Her overburdened mind could not handle even one more torturous memory. She went about her daily duties with Nalehileehque as if nothing had happened. Her adopted mother said nothing either which made it easier for Penelope to forget the things she saw and heard that night.

She continued to pray for rescue, and although she felt her prayers were being heard, she had really given up on the prospect of living among her kind again. Her adopted family asked about her God and she tried as best she could to explain. They, too, believed in only one God, but they believed He took many forms. It was difficult for each side to grasp the religion of the other, but neither side ridiculed the other's beliefs. Penelope tried desperately to live as a missionary should by showing kindness to those around her. She hoped that she could lead others to Christ by example.

She was learning the Lenape language almost as fast as they were learning English. Owehela had insisted that every member of his family learn from Penelope. So, she taught them English and as much of the white mannerisms as she could. Nalehileehque taught her about a woman's role in their society as well. It was not long before she came to realize how extremely intelligent these people were. They learned quickly and easily, not at all like the stories she had been told about these "savages." However, the stories about them being nearly naked were true. Somehow, though, their nakedness did not seem to bother her when put into the context of everything else around her.

The Lenape had tried to live in peace with the whites, although the Europeans had made it very difficult. Times had been especially harsh since Kieft had taken charge. The whites began to take advantage in trades and treat the natives with little or no respect. The customs and treaties that had been established earlier were abandoned with his administration. The hatred of Kieft was growing and the surrounding tribes were getting tired of the bad treatment they felt they were receiving. War was being raged all around them and there was not much they could do about it except to fight back.

A few months ago a young Indian had killed a wheelwright in New Amsterdam by nearly cutting off his head. The killing appeared to be unprovoked, but word had gotten out that this young man was seeking revenge for the brutal murder of his uncle twenty years ago which he thought was unjustified. The young Indian had fled the town and was now roaming the countryside, avoiding the Dutch. Kieft vowed that he would get justice and demanded that the Indians in the area turn him in for trial. However, the Indians would not betray their own, even if he was not of their particular tribe. They did not trust this Kieft and would not comply with his demands believing that the score was settled. Kieft, in turn, went on a rampage with his latest massacres, killing even those that had nothing to do with any of it, many times waiting until the men of the villages were away in hunting parties before killing the women and children.

However, their trouble was not only with the invasion of the whites, it was also with other overbearing tribes. The Mohawks had received favored privileges from the director general in the fur trade. That, they felt, garnished them some sort of importance over the

CHAPTER 8

other tribes. They would come to Owehela's village every so often and demand tribute as a subsidy for their protection.

The Lenape did not like the Mohawks, but being as they were usually a negotiable people, they tried to appease the warlords as much as possible. They even took the verbal abuse the Mohawks heaped on them for holding peace so dear. They took great joy in calling the Lenape "old women" or "the grandfathers," making fun of their past as peacekeepers. The whole name for the Lenape tribe was Lenni Lenape which means "real men." They did not view the Mohawks as men, but as not much more than animals, powerful animals, but still lower than real men. The Lenape viewed negotiation and communication as something of which to be proud, a sign of strength and wisdom, always trying the peaceful way first. The Mohawks viewed it as weakness.

Penelope grew to love her adopted family and appreciate their ways. She adopted their way of dressing, finding it much freer than the way she had grown up knowing. She wore outfits much like Nalehileehque, a dress worn over long breeches. (She never adopted the nakedness, however. It was more than her moral upbringing could bear.) It was because of the love and loyalty she felt towards these people that she was able to block out the episodes of what she perceived as cruelty they sometimes committed. As much as she loved them all, a part of her still missed the world she was familiar with.

One fall day she was returning to Owehela's house with squash she had just gathered from their garden when she saw three white men talking to Tateuscung. She could not hear their conversation as she was not yet close enough. She did not know two of the men, but one looked familiar. When she came closer she noticed that one of the men looked very much like the Captain who had left her on the beach to die.

Her heart beat hard in her chest and her feet went from merely walking to stomping. She did not realize that her face had turned into a scowl as her determined steps brought her closer to the group of men. She felt her face grow flush as every ounce of raw, pure, unadulterated hatred flooded her very being. She moved faster and faster until she dropped her squash and ran to the man who had caused her the greatest pain of her young life and began to hit him hard with her good right arm and attempted to hit him with her left. She slapped and scratched him and hit his chest as the poor man stood there and took the beating. Jacobson just stood there as she cursed him and tried her best to hurt him.

His chest, sides, and broken nose already hurt from the beating he took last night, but he felt she probably deserved to do whatever she wanted to him. Somehow her blows eased his guilt. So, he stood there tall and stone faced, not moving as Penelope cried and beat him. She wanted him to die in a painful way and to feel the hurt that her body and soul had felt. She wanted revenge for Kent and justification for herself, all the while hating herself for the rage inside her. For more than a year the passionate hatred had burned and she had kept it back. The floodgates finally broke loose at the very site of this wretched man.

Stout, realizing what was going on and that these two obviously knew each other stepped in between his friend and the crazy woman. He took hold of her hands and pushed her back, causing her head covering to slide down the back of her head, revealing her terrible scar. Horrified at her exposure, she quickly grabbed her covering and ran into the hut, humiliated and angry that she could not kill the object of her hatred.

"Well, I guess that answers that," said Stout to his friend. "She is definitely the woman we are searching for if she has a reaction like that."

"That was the baroness. I almost didn't recognize her." Jacobson said with a crack in his voice, obviously disturbed by the way she now looked. He didn't cry, but he had a lump in his throat the size of McPherson's fist.

"I can see ye have a way with women," said McPherson jokingly trying to lighten the mood.

"Do you know this woman?" Tateuscung demanded to know.

The men looked at Jacobson. He did not know where the scars had

CHAPTER 8

come from or if these people did it to her, but he was going to find out. What had happened to this woman? What had he done? He mustered his voice from somewhere deep within.

"That is Baroness Van Princes. She was a passenger on my ship last year. We have been searching for her."

"It appears that she does not want you to search for her," Tateuscung said harshly. He did not like this man after seeing Penelope's reaction to him. Having grown to love her like a sister, he would kill anyone he felt threatened her.

"What have you done to her?!" Jacobson demanded to know.

"We have done nothing to her. She was upset over the site of you! What did you do to her?!" was the response.

Richard realized that negotiations might get tedious with this line of communication so he had to think quickly. "It is just that the baroness did not have these scars the last time Captain Jacobson saw her. He is worried about her and wants to make sure she is all right," he said as he stepped in between the two men, again saving his friend from another thrashing.

McPherson, being friends with Tateuscung, asked "we would like to see if the woman is the same one we are looking for, that's all." He was trying to relieve the tension that had built.

"Would it be all right if I spoke with her?" asked Stout of Tateuscung.

Tateuscung had not taken his eyes off of Jacobson. This man had better not move an inch, because that is all would take to make the young Indian kill him. Penelope would not be harmed again.

Finally, after a long pause, Tateuscung looked to Stout who had asked the question. Tateuscung thought for a moment how this would probably be better handled by his father. After another pause he spoke "my father Owehela will be home soon. I will speak to him about this. He will decide."

"Thank you," said Stout. "We will camp by the stream if that is all right. You can find us there when your father gets back."

Tateuscung nodded. He kept a watchful glare on the men as they mounted their horses and left the village. He would inform Owehela when he got back from fishing about what had happened.

"I told you she was damaged," said McPherson in a matter of fact manner.

"You didn't say she had been scalped! What in God's name has she been through? Blasted savages, always scalping!" said Jacobson.

McPherson's temper emerged. "These people did no' know about scalping until the white man came along! Your damnable Kieft has been paying rewards to those who bring in Indian scalps. The Indians learned fast that the white man considered them trophies, so now they take them as trophies of their own."

Stout paid no attention to the conversation between the other two men. He was still amazed at the woman's spirit and said "that woman has been to Hell and back, yet she still had enough fight in her to take you on, Jacobson. Amazing!"

Jacobson thought about the fortitude, or was it stupidity, she had shown when he last saw her. He remembered the beautiful young woman standing there on the beach, over her husband, jaw stuck out in defiance. That image had haunted him all these months, only to be substituted in his nightmares by images of what could have been done to her after he left. His nightmares had probably been more gracious that reality.

"You don't know that woman, Stout. She would take on a badger if she thought she was right. Maybe this was not such a good idea after all. Perhaps we should just go if she is that crazy. She is even worse than I remember. Maybe the Indian lifestyle has made her go insane and we should just leave now."

McPherson was incensed again by the Captain's words. "What do ye mean 'the Indian lifestyle has made her go insane'? I have lived among the Indians for better than twenty years and I am here to tell ye. It is not the Indian lifestyle that makes a man go insane. It would be the white one. The Indians are simple people with simple pleasures, enjoying life as they live it. Our so called 'civilization' with all its pressures and structures and laws and such pile too much stress on a mind. That would be what makes a man go insane!"

"I merely meant that, perhaps with all she has been through, she

CHAPTER 8

doesn't need to go back to a society where people might not understand the way she looks." Jacobson was trying to be kind; he was just not using the right words.

"Why don't we let the woman decide for herself what she wants to do? I will speak with her as soon as possible. If nothing else I can find out what happened to her. She has some kind of fortitude to have that kind of spirit after all she has been through. I was not expecting this," Stout said.

"That young Indian back there…" Jacobson began.

McPherson interrupted "his name is Tateuscung. He is Agnes' cousin."

"Tateuscung" he said hard and toward McPherson "did not like me. I don't know that the old man will either. I know Penelope was not happy to see me. What will happen to us if they decide they don't want to let her go? Will they even let US go?"

"Ye worry too much" said McPherson.

"Look at you. Of course YOU are not worried. You are part of their family. We are not. You might even help them torture us!" Jacobson replied to the Scotsman.

"Believe me," said McPherson sternly and with a squint in his bloodshot eye "if they wanted to do me in, they would not let a little thing like family stop them. Owehela is a smart man. He will listen and make up his mind."

"I certainly hope so. I would like to know what has happened to this woman," said Stout.

Penelope, meanwhile, was in Owehela's house distracting herself with any type of work she could find. She was first trying to finish the weave she had started, then she started cooking, and then she would weave some more. She could think of nothing but her hatred for the man she had just seen. She spoke nothing to Nalehileehque or anyone else for that matter the rest of the evening. She wallowed in the anger and bitterness that consumed her since its release.

The next morning Owehela called to Penelope. "Who is this man that angered you?"

"He is the captain of the ship my husband and I were on."

"Is he the one who hurt you?" Owehela needed to know if the man needed killing.

Penelope looked down as she answered. "No, he is not one of the men who attacked me. He is the one who left us there on the beach to die."

"But you did not die" he reasoned. "You lived and he has returned."

Penelope looked directly at her friend. "Yes, I lived, but my husband did not. That man left my sick husband and me to die on that beach without looking back. He said he would return for us, but he did not. Because of him I now carry these scars and have little use of my arm."

"Are you angry because he did not return soon enough or are you angry because he left in the first place?"

"Both" she said.

"But if he had not left you, we would not have found you. And if we had not found you, we could not have learned to speak the language you have taught us. Is that not so?"

She realized that he was being logical and she had no ambition for logic right now. She fed on her cancerous hatred, but his words cut her straight to her heart. Yes, she had been through more than she could have ever imagined. Yes, she became a widow and nearly died. But, if she had not been left on that beach she would not have met precious Nalehileehque or Tateuscung or Owehela or the others. Her anger diminished somewhat. Was this part of God's plan all along? Did she have to suffer this much to find a mother she never had? She had to think…and pray.

The three men camped by the stream all that afternoon and into the next morning. They had brought with them two extra horses loaded with supplies, tobacco, and wampum just in case they needed to trade. Perhaps just the temptation of a trade that good would be enough to convince the old man to at least listen to the proposal.

Late the next afternoon Tateuscung sent his younger brother to get the men. "Owehela said you may come speak to him now" said

CHAPTER 8

the ten year old to the white men. "Come with me."

Jacobson and Stout looked at each other in wonder. They had never heard an Indian child speak English so well. It was an odd site for them to see a nearly naked brown-skinned child speak anything but his native tongue. Obviously, Penelope had been busy while she was here.

The men followed the child back to Owehela's house. The old man and Tateuscung were waiting for them at the fire outside. Penelope and Nalehileehque sat behind them.

"Sit down. Would you like something to eat?" Owehela asked.

Jacobson was amazed at the manners of this savage. McPherson was not. He knew the Lenape to be hospitable people, always offering guests food if it was available. Agnes' family had always been kind to him. Stout could not help but watch Penelope, not paying attention to much else. He was not staring at her scars, but at the beauty he saw inside her.

Stout realized that Owehela had spoken to him and pulled his eyes back to the old Indian. "Thank you. We would be honored to eat with you." He knew that to turn down an invitation to eat would be an insult. Besides, Stout also knew that McPherson never wanted to turn down food, any food.

Penelope and Nalehileehque prepared a bowl of food for each of the men and brought it to them. Penelope handed Stout and McPherson each a bowl with no expression at all on her face. Knowing of Penelope's hatred for him, Nalehileehque took care of Jacobson so that Penelope did not have to. By now all of Owehela's family knew that Captain Jacobson was the one who left Penelope and Kent vulnerable on the beach and how she felt about him.

After their meal Stout began negotiations with Owehela. "The lady Penelope Van Princes is a white woman. We understand that she came to you last year in distress. We have been looking for her all this time. We would like to ask if there is a way that you would let her go back to our people with us."

Owehela thought for a moment and then answered "that would be a decision Penelope has to make. If she wants to go with you, it is good. If she wants to stay with us, it is good."

Richard did not think the prospect of her going with them looked promising at the moment so he asked "would it be acceptable to you if I spoke with Penelope privately before she makes the decision?"

Owehela, always deliberate, looked at a stoic Penelope and then back to the men without any emotion. "You may speak with her, but she is the one who will decide."

"Thank you."

All three men got up to speak with Penelope. McPherson and Jacobson were stopped by Tateuscung. "Only this one may speak with her" he said as he stepped in front of the two men. Looking sternly at Jacobson he said "you must wait."

Richard and Penelope walked to a tree well within site of the group of negotiators. Richard, already enamored with this woman, tried to show restraint and composure. He felt like he was twenty again instead of in his forties. Jacobson's story had been true. This woman really existed and was standing right in front of him. He had already seen her scar, but right now all he saw was her beauty.

"Hello. My name is Richard Stout."

"And you know I am Penelope Van Princes." She was cautious because she did not know this man and he was with that traitorous captain.

"We have come to take you back to New Amsterdam if you wish to go."

"So I heard. Why did it take you so long to find me? Why didn't the captain send a rescue party back for us like he said he would?"

Stout understood her questioning of him. He could see where she would feel abandoned and betrayed by the very ones who were now here to save her. "Captain Jacobson did send a rescue party back to you after he got everyone to New Amsterdam safely," he said. "When they returned to the landing they only found your husband's body and bloody blankets. They assumed that you were dead, too. We only learned of a white woman living with Indians recently and that is why we came. We needed to find out if the woman was you. Lucky for us, it was you."

CHAPTER 8

"But, why didn't he just take Kent and me with him on that day? Why do you want me to come with you now?" she had so many questions and could not get them all out.

"He told me that he could not, as much as he wanted to do that, he could not. To save Kent would mean killing the other people. He could not risk the lives of so many for the life of just one. It has been a decision he has struggled with since that day and it was not one made easily."

"It did not look to me like he had a difficult time making it" she said sternly.

"It may not have looked that way, but he did. He did not want to make that decision, but he had to. He had to save as many people as he could. He would have saved you, too, if you had gone with him." Richard tried to reason with her.

"I could not leave my husband!" Penelope was still adamant about that. "He was sick. I had to stay with him."

"Yes, I know. Believe me, it was a noble thing to do. I have never heard of anything so noble…"

"I was not being noble" she spouted. "I loved my husband and he needed me. I could not leave him."

"Yes, I understand. Captain Jacobson regrets all that has happened. He would change things if he could. We all would. But, we can't so you must start from right here, right now with your decision."

Penelope was confused. This was the moment she had been hoping and praying for ever since that day on the beach. Why was she being so stubborn about it now? Why wasn't she happier to see these men who had come for her?

She realized that to go with these men meant that she may or may not be accepted by the "civilized" society. She was not pitied by the family she lived with now, but would she be pitied in the white New Amsterdam? Would she be accepted again after living with the so-called savages for so long? Why would she want to put herself through the agony of starting over? Hadn't she just spent the last year or so of her life doing just that, starting over? Her moment of salvation was here, but she was scared inside. She would not let this stranger see her feelings, though.

"Baroness, we don't want to hurt you. We want you to come back to New Amsterdam with us. Captain Jacobson has lived in torment ever since he came back from the rescue attempt. Don't let him suffer anymore. Ease his conscience and rest his mind" Stout reasoned.

"Rest his mind! Why should I rest HIS mind? It was because of him that I wear these scars," she said, knowing that he had seen her head earlier. She held out her left arm to show the damage. "Mr. Stout, my sick husband and I were left on the beach after the shipwreck to die by that wretched man because we were too much of a burden for him! He chose to leave us there unprotected. We were attacked and Kent died. I was scalped, cut, brutalized and left for dead. These people in this village saved me, which is more than I can say for the white people who left me. Why would I leave these people who have been kind to me to return to a society that has not? It would have been kinder of that captain had he just killed us both before he went on to New Amsterdam."

Penelope looked sternly into Richard's face as she spewed the words out of her mouth. This past year had freed her from the inhibitions of her upbringing. She had no trouble at all this time standing up to a man. Her hatred of Jacobson and Richard's companionship with him had blinded her to anything good, even his good intentions.

She stopped and reflected on what she had just said. The words felt like they were coming from someone else. She had felt so angry for so long that she could not contain her emotions and she did not like the way she was sounding, but she could not stop. She had almost given in to the softening of her heart, but the anger was just too great.

"Baroness, we want you to come with us. When I heard what happened I admired your loyalty to your husband. Now that I have met you for myself I see now why Jacobson speaks of you with such admiration."

"Ha. Admiration? I doubt that" she said in a mocking tone, her emotions so burning that her knees shook and her body trembled. She

CHAPTER 8

still did not like the words coming out of her own mouth. She paused and looked at this stranger for a moment. For only a moment she let herself notice that he had kind eyes.

Richard seemed sincere, but was he? Why should she ease Jacobson's mind? Had he really even thought about her during her turmoil? She had not seen anything on the ship that had shown he had a conscience.

"We must go back now" was her reply.

Richard felt his heart sink. Here was a woman who had more conviction than anyone he had ever heard of. She was fearless, or so she seemed. He could not believe that she would rather stay with these people than return to her own kind. Yet, he understood the feelings of betrayal and how intense they could be and how long one could harbor them.

"Very well, as you wish," he said.

The couple returned to the group around the fire. While Richard and Penelope were talking McPherson had given Nalehileehque the sack of sugar that Agnes had sent to her. It was customary for gifts to be given by the visitors to the host.

Owehela spoke first to Penelope when they got back. "What have you decided? Do you wish to return with them or do you wish to stay here at my home?"

Penelope thought for a moment about the whirlwind around her. She loved these people very much and would always be grateful for everything they had done for her and had given to her. She finally had a wonderful mother in Nalehileehque.

But, this was the moment she had been praying for. If she passed this opportunity up, one may never come again. If she did not go now she would be giving up the chance to know the very reason that her father sent her here in the first place. She felt sick to her stomach.

After a long pause she spoke. "Owehela, Nalehileehque, I love you very much and I appreciate all you have done for me. But, if it is all right with you, I would like to go to New Amsterdam with them."

The old couple looked at each other in disbelief. They had not expected Penelope to go with the men, but to stay in the safety of their home. The three white men were also amazed at her decision. She had not given any indication to Stout that she even wanted to go with them, in fact, just the opposite.

Trying not to look disappointed Owehela said "if that is what you wish, you may go."

McPherson knew that to keep good relations meant that gifts must be given in trade. The Indian man had done a gracious thing which traditionally must be followed by giving of gifts, so he spoke. "We thank ye for the woman. We have brought gifts for ye kindness."

He motioned for Jacobson to go get the supplies. Jacobson got up and brought back the two beautiful roan mares they had brought with them to trade that were loaded with trading gifts. McPherson took the reigns and handed them to Owehela who took them with a nod. He was happy for the gifts, but he would miss Penelope. He did not feel betrayed by her decision, however. He knew that she wanted to get back to her life.

They all stayed and ate supper there with Owehela and his family that night. The next morning the group of white travelers pointed their horses toward their world.

Chapter 9

New Amsterdam

Lady Moody was determined to see director general Kieft. The attack last week had been unprovoked and now Gravesend needed help with defense. They had done well protecting themselves, but how long could they keep it up? He would just have to spare some of his military to help defend against the Indians who were unusually aggressive. She would just have to convince him that their safety depended upon his help.

William Bowne, the justice of the peace for Gravesend, had agreed to accompany her to speak with Kieft. Bowne was as good a man as he was impressive looking. He was broad shouldered and strong jawed. Standing at 6'2" he carried a presence and was as tolerant and fair a man as Lady Deborah had ever encountered. He was Richard Stout's best friend and served also as an unofficial preacher at times. He had earned the trust of all those in Gravesend and had a reputation for being open minded and tolerant of faiths other than his own.

"I don't know, Lady Deborah, if Kieft will send help to us at Gravesend" said Bowne. "He has his troops scattered trying to put out rebellions all over."

Lady Deborah was annoyed at the director general, but tried not to show it. "Yes, I know, but we have to ask. If we don't ask for help we certainly won't get it."

"You are right, of course. I just don't see the director general caring at all about our situation." Browne had known Kieft a long time and thought very little of him.

"All we can do is ask and hope," she said.

"And pray," he added.

"Yes and pray."

The carriage in which they were riding finally made it to the gates of the town. The streets were busier and more populated than usual. Neither William nor Lady Deborah remembered so many people living in town the last time they had visited. Obviously, the Indian wars had sent the white people looking for safety and this was their harbor. Kieft had made sure he was going to be safe, even if no one else was. He doubled the troops inside the town and set up permanent guard posts outside his house and office.

The two Gravesenders went inside the director general's office to speak with him. They did not have an appointment, but Lady Deborah could usually get in to speak with Kieft unannounced. He had grown fond of Lady Deborah because she had become one of only a few people left who made a genuine effort to be courteous to him. He was getting used to people, especially the patentees, telling him how ridiculous he was.

Bowne announced their presence and their request for an audience with the director general to the secretary in the front office. The young man took down the information that Mr. Bowne gave him and assured them that he would make sure Mr. Kieft got the message. He informed them that the director general was out of the office at the moment, but had plans to return that afternoon. They could stay or come back at 2:00. Bowne looked outside to the large clock on the town hall and saw that the time was only 11:00.

Turning to Lady Moody he inquired if she would like to eat lunch while they waited. She agreed and they stepped out of the dark office

CHAPTER 9

into the sunshine outside. They walked across the street just in time to see Richard Stout and Captain Jacobson coming into town with a strange woman riding behind Stout on his horse. McPherson had gone to his house instead of coming to town with them.

The young woman interested both Bowne and Lady Moody, but most especially Lady Moody. She was dressed like an Indian woman, but was obviously white. This was a site that both of the onlookers naturally had to investigate.

"Hello Richard!" yelled Bowne to his friend, motioning for him to come over.

Richard saw his friends, tipped his hat, and yelled back his greeting "Hello!" He led his entourage over to where Bowne and Lady Moody were standing.

Amazed, but trying not to look like they were gawking, the two well dressed dignitaries smiled. Bowne had known Stout a long time and thought he would never again be surprised by anything he did. Stout was always trying out different inventions and new ideas. Today, however, he had managed to surprise even Bowne.

Tipping their hats to Lady Deborah, Richard and the Captain dismounted. Richard helped Penelope off afterwards. Lady Deborah could not stand it any longer. She just had to find out who the strange woman was.

"Who do you have with you today, Mr. Stout?"

"William Bowne, Lady Deborah Moody, allow me to introduce to you my friend Captain Danel Jacobson."

Bowne shook his hand and Lady Deborah curtsied in fine manner.

"Mr. Bowne and Lady Moody, this is Baroness Penelope Van Princes."

"Baroness?" said Lady Moody surprised.

Bowne tipped his hat and Lady Deborah curtsied again to which Penelope curtsied in return. This site had just become even more strange, a white woman with a colorful headdress in Indian clothing just curtsied in court-like manner to a man and a woman. People on the street were now beginning to stare.

Noticing the attention they were garnishing Bowne said "We were just about to have lunch. Would you care to join us?"

"Yes, thank you. I am very hungry. How about you two?" Richard turned to Penelope and Jacobson.

Both nodded and the group entered the pub that also served as a restaurant. They had just become an even odder looking group of people. Here was a man and a woman dressed in their finest garments in the company of a white woman in Indian clothing and two men in tattered traveling clothes. It was a motley crew, but all held their heads high as if their appearances were perfectly normal. In a town so diverse as to have eighteen different languages spoken, it would seem that almost any site looked normal, but not this one.

They sat down at a table toward the back of the room. Stout knew that his friend was so curious about Penelope that he was about to pop his immaculately knotted neck tie. He grinned at the thought of that actually happening. Lady Deborah, as much as she tried to conceal it, was just as curious as her escort.

"Tell me news of home" Richard began as if nothing had happened to him in the past several days and before William and Lady Moody could ask any more questions. He wanted them to wait a little longer for any answers they might desire.

"That's why we are here," Said Bowne, still trying to keep his eyes from wondering back to Penelope. "We had the worst Indian attack yet last week. They came at night when they thought we were asleep. Looked like Raritan, the same as those that have attacked and killed the Hollanders in surrounding settlements."

Lady Moody broke in "thank God, we found out about the attack in time to stop it. My son has an Indian friend who warned us in time to prepare."

Lady Moody stopped and looked at Penelope who was trying to get her bearings again in a white society. Could this be the woman who taught Tateuscung to speak English? No, that was impossible...wasn't it? Surely this could not be such a coincidence.

Penelope tried to listen to the conversation that was going on at the table, but her mind was distracted. She had almost forgotten what

CHAPTER 9

it felt like to be surrounded by her own kind. Today she didn't feel like she was one of them. She felt like she was some kind of oddity, not white, but not native either. Suddenly she felt very uneasy and anxious and very conscious of her dress. She touched her head dress to make sure everything was in place, smoothed her dress in her lap, and looked down to make sure her ankles were still covered. Once she had been very comfortable in a crowded setting, but not today. Anxiety was gnawing at her and causing her stomach to flip.

"Is everyone all right? Was anyone hurt? Did they burn anything?" Richard became instantly serious.

"Everyone is fine, just shaken. We managed to kill several of them before they finally retreated. We must have gotten them before they could get to the buildings and livestock" William assured him.

"That's why we're here today. We came to ask Mr. Kieft to send a few of his troops to help us protect Gravesend. We want to make sure that we have reinforcements in case there is a next time" said Lady Moody.

"Oh I am sure there will be a next time" said Bowne.

"There will be if they think you are unprotected" said Jacobson.

"We are supposed to meet with the director general at 2:00 to ask for his help. Would you like to go to the meeting, Richard?" Bowne asked.

"I certainly would."

Lady Moody had not lost her curiosity about Penelope. She turned to this strange looking woman beside her and asked "and where are you from, dear?" but she really wanted to ask so much more.

Realizing that the beautiful woman was speaking to her, Penelope looked back around to her and said "I am from Holland."

"Holland? That is not an answer I would have guessed. You sound English."

"My parents moved from England to Holland before I was born. I speak both Dutch and English."

Noticing how uncomfortable Penelope had become, Richard answered. "The baroness and her husband were shipwrecked. The baron, regretfully, died. Captain Jacobson and I found her a couple of days ago. She was living with some of the Indians south of here. You remember Benjamin McPherson, the trader? The baroness was staying with some of his wife's relatives while she healed from some injuries she sustained."

"Oh you poor thing!" said Lady Deborah.

That was it, the thing most dreaded by Penelope, pity. She could stand the stares, the questions, anything but pity. Why do people think that they should feel sorry for someone?

"Yes, well…" Penelope started, and then looked to Richard for help.

"Penelope has learned some of the Indian language while she was in their company. She told me that they call themselves Lenape, but we call them Delaware. She even managed to teach some of them our language."

Suddenly Lady Moody's pity changed to admiration. "That is wonderful! You turned a terrible situation into something very positive. The young Indian man who warned us of the impending attack spoke English very well. His name is Tateuscung and he said he had a woman teacher who lived with his family. Do you know him?"

"Yes. He and his father saved my life. They took me back to their home and his family took care of me after my husband and I were attacked." She stared hard at Jacobson, who hung his head so that he could not see her eyes. Penelope had tolerated the horrid man to get to New Amsterdam, but she did not want to converse with him. She also did not want to reveal the other details of her ordeal to these new people. She had just had to relive the whole thing a few days ago and the re-opened psychological wounds hurt too much.

Richard could see that this conversation was bothering his two friends so he changed the subject back to the attacks. "I think we will find it very hard to persuade Kieft to send us any protection."

"That is exactly what I think," said Bowne. "We must be prepared to defend ourselves, at least until Kieft is relieved of office."

"What do you mean 'relieved of office'" asked Jacobson.

CHAPTER 9

"Mr. Kieft has made many of the men in his own administration angry. They blame him for the problems we have. Just look around this town. Have you noticed how many grog shops have gone up since last year? It is getting ridiculous!" Bowne replied.

"The only person inside the gated walls of this fort who tolerates Mr. Kieft these days is Parson Bogardus, and that is only because of the new church that Kieft had built to get the Parson from preaching Hell fire and damnation down on him. Old Bogardus just loves preaching from that new pulpit!" Richard smiled. He knew how Bowne felt about Bogardus and laughed under his breath as Bowne rolled his eyes.

They finished with their lunch, passing the time until 2:00 came. Jacobson wanted to get down to the harbor to see about his new ship. It would be sailing back to Holland in a couple of days and he wanted to make sure everything was satisfactorily supplied and check on the new crew. He pulled Stout aside as the others were leisurely walking back to the director general's office.

"I can't thank you enough for what you have done" he told Stout.

"You don't owe me any thanks. We just went looking to find out what happened to one of your unfortunate passengers."

"Yes and I can go on with my life now. She is not the same, but she is alive and at least I know that." He handed Stout a small purse with coins in it. "Here, take this and buy the Baroness a new dress and help her get started again. It's not much, but it is all I have saved over the past year. She deserves more, but it is all I have. You will help her find a place to stay?"

Richard took the purse and replied "yes, of course. But, why don't you take care of this matter yourself. Give her a chance to forgive you."

"No. I think it better this way. I can understand her hatred of me. I even hate myself for what has happened. Although, I can at least face a mirror now that I know she will be taken care of" said the captain with a half-hearted smile.

"I will keep in touch. Everything will be all right now."

The two men parted company, each to greet his life with a

renewed respect and appreciation for the unpredictable times in which they lived. It would be the last time they saw each other. Jacobson set sail for Holland, settled down there and raised a family. He learned over time to forgive himself a little, but he always had the feisty young scalped woman in the back of his mind.

Richard entered Kieft's office and saw that Penelope was waiting with the secretary. She sat in a chair by the window and watched as the people went by. She listened to the languages, took in the smells, and tried to get acclimated to this type of society again. Already she missed her surrogate family. She did not see Richard come through the office. The secretary motioned him go on to the director general's office.

Richard entered shortly after Lady Moody and Bowne. Only the pleasantries had been exchanged. "To what do I owe the pleasure of your visit, Lady Moody?" asked Kieft with a sugary sweet tone that he reserved only for her. Of all the people he knew, hers was the only respect he wanted.

"We have come to ask for your help, sir" began Lady Deborah, getting straight to the point. "As you know the Indians have become quite aggressive lately. They have attacked several of the settlements in our surrounding area, killing, burning, and destroying practically everything around us. They even tried to attack Gravesend last week in the dark of night. Fortunately, we were able to repulse the attack."

"Yes, so I heard" said Kieft in a manner that was too calm for Bowne and Stout who did not trust the man and assumed he was up to something. "You defended yourselves quite admirably against the aborigines, I have been told." He loved that word—aborigine. It made the opponent sound so, so, so…barbaric.

Bowne could not hold back any longer "we have come to ask you to help us defend ourselves. We need for you to send a few soldiers to our settlement to help us protect our families and property. You have many guards in this fort and many surrounding it. Surely you could help us by sending a few to help us, your patentees, if for nothing else but to protect your investment."

Kieft sat there in his chair, eyebrows raised in mock astonishment

CHAPTER 9

that these good people would ask for his help. He was too calm. Stout knew he was up to something now. Saying nothing, Stout studied the politician's face while Bowne and Lady Moody explained their needs to him. Something was going on.

After they had finished making their case for protection, Kieft got up from his chair and walked over to his window to act as if he was looking out. In reality, he was only turning his smirking face away from the unsuspecting victims.

"I wish I could help you" he began "but I have some even more distressing news. In fact, I was going to send a messenger out to Gravesend today. We have to recall the men of your settlement to New Amsterdam to help protect the fort. These uprisings have gotten out of hand and we need all the men we can get."

Stout had known he was up to something. "You can't do that! We have families, homes, property there. We cannot leave our homes to come protect yours."

"You don't have a choice" Kieft smirked. "If you want to keep your charter, you must be recalled to military service."

"You would revoke our charter?" asked Lady Deborah. "Why would you do that?"

"Because, madam, we are at war. War requires men to fight. You are under the protection of the Dutch; the Dutch are at war with the aborigines; we need the men to fight, so there you are. It is that simple. I am sorry about your settlement. It will just have to wait until after peace is established."

"That is not right and you know it. We should be protecting our interests, not yours. Besides, I have seen the number of troops that you have. You don't need to recall those who have already served! We should be required to defend the interests there, in Gravesend." Stout shouted. He was not a shouting man, but he was angry at this bureaucrat.

"I am not going to argue with you about it. Since you are here, you may take the proclamation back to your settlement for the men to come back here for their duty papers." Kieft was cold blooded. He did not look at Lady Moody even once during his little announcement. She had steely eyes and he knew that one defiant look from her would be worse than one of Parson Bogardus' sermons about Hell fire.

"We will defy it. We will stay and defend our interests in our own homes!" shouted Bowne.

"You do that" said Kieft in almost a growl "and you won't have to worry about the aborigines burning your homes and killing your people. I will have it done!"

Realizing that theirs was a losing battle the three angry petitioners readied to leave this worthless human being's office. Lady Deborah could not help herself. She was determined to tell him what she thought. Getting up from her chair she walked over to the window where Kieft had planted himself. She stood right in front of him and said "look at me." He would not. "LOOK AT ME!" she demanded. Finally, reluctantly, the coward turned and faced her.

"This war would never have started if it had not been for you, you pathetic little man. You are the reason so many have died needlessly. Now, you are leaving the women and children of Gravesend defenseless against a brutal enemy just so your sorry self can be protected. Shame and damnation to you." Lady Moody stopped being courteous and mannerly and went straight to how she felt. She was past the point of no return in her anger. "Our men will honor the recall and they will serve admirably and we women will do our best to keep things right at home, but I want you to know that you are not worth the life of even one of our dogs!"

Stout and Bowne raised their eyebrows and looked at each other for they had never heard Lady Moody speak this way. They knew that she had just put into words everything they were feeling. Taking their cue from her they exited with a hard slam to his office door.

Penelope had heard the shouting in the office and stood closer to the door to hear. When Richard, William, and Lady Moody came out she fell in line with them. They gathered their horses and their carriage and left together with heavy hearts to return to Gravesend with a message from the director general.

Chapter 10

Kieft's War

Lady Moody, William Bowne, Richard Stout, and Penelope Van Princes arrived at Gravesend with heavy hearts and solemn faces. They had hoped to bring supporting troops back with them or at least the good news that troops were on their way. Instead, they had the treacherous task of reporting that Director General Kieft had not only denied them aid, but had even recalled the Gravesend men to the Dutch military service.

As soon as the group arrived at Lady Moody's house she immediately dispatched Henry to tell the neighbors that there was to be an emergency town meeting at her house in two hours. It was absolutely essential that everyone attend.

William went immediately to his house to tell his wife Ann what had happened and to prepare for his family's removal to a safer location. They had four boys, thirteen year old John, seven year old James, five year old Andrew, and three year old Philip. A separation during this time in his family's life would be especially hard on Ann.

While Henry was away on his assignment the remaining adults sat down to eat for lunch. They ate their meal in almost total silence at Lady Moody's kitchen table. Frieda had prepared fish, beans, and corn.

After lunch, while they were waiting for everyone to arrive, Richard took an opportunity to speak privately with Lady Deborah. He escorted her to the dock in a walk to try to calm nerves. He told her of the past few days' events and of Penelope's story as told to him by Captain Jacobson.

"I need your help, Lady Moody" said Richard after the tale was told. "I had intended on allowing the baroness to stay at my residence until such time as we could contact her family, if she has any. But, now that I have been recalled that plan must be changed."

"Yes, I see" said Lady Moody. "Does the baroness have any family here in the New World?"

"I don't know yet. The baroness has spoken very little since we left the Indian village where she was staying. I had intended on trying to find out more once she was settled in and had a chance to get used to all of us."

Lady Moody was a generous and kind person, but more than that she was almost as curious about this wonderfully enigmatic woman as Stout was. "Mr. Stout, I will be glad to allow the baroness to live with me until you can return to us. Hopefully, by then we will know more of her family situation."

"Thank you, Lady Moody" said Richard. "Your compassion is only exceeded by your beauty." With that, he took off his hat, bowed, and kissed her hand. Lady Moody loved this kind of attention. She could see right through any rogue who had before tried to flatter her, but Stout was different. He was sincere in what he thought and his gratitude was genuine. She appreciated his sincerity and it made the gesture even more appreciated.

"Captain Jacobson sent this money for the baroness' care." He handed her the small purse. "He asked that she have new clothes. Use this for any expenses that you might incur on her behalf. If you need more, please keep a record and I will pay when I see you next."

Lady Moody took the purse and said "I am sure that whatever is in this purse will adequately take care of everything. I will see to her

CHAPTER 10

clothing as soon as possible. Captain Jacobson is a generous man."

"Yes he is. More than that, however, he is a man who feels responsibility for what happened to her. He is a good man who was put in a difficult situation and is now living with the consequences of it. Fortunately, we were able to find the baroness. If we had not, I don't know what would have happened to him."

"Well, happily for all of us, you found her. I am anxious to get acquainted with Baroness Van Princes. The timing today was just not good" said Lady Moody with a sigh. The two turned from the dock and started walking back to Lady Deborah's house where a crowd of people was beginning to gather.

William Bowne and Richard Stout called the meeting to order. They told of the meeting with the director general and about the recall. Sergeant James Hubbard and Ensign George Baxter were the most incensed. "We are English. How can the Dutch do this to us?" they yelled. "We have already served our time in the military!"

"Yes, we explained all that and how our families needed us to stay here" said Bowne. "It made no difference to Kieft. The situation is: we either go in for the recall to duty or loose the charter. It is that simple."

"He cannot do that! He has no right to deny our charter! Most of us have already paid last year's tithe on this property!" said Nicholas Stillwell, equally outraged.

Richard broke in "he can and he will. He threatened to burn us out himself if we refuse to help in his war with the natives."

"What we need to decide is how best to protect our families while the men are away" said William Bowne. "I would suggest that those who have homes in New Amsterdam should take their families there where the protection is the best."

"Fort Amserfoort in the flatlands is also well protected" said Lady Moody.

"Very well" said Stout. "We don't need to leave anyone here to try to defend Gravesend alone. It is very important that all of us seek shelter for our families." He looked at Penelope knowing what kind of psychological damage could be done to someone left behind or to the someone doing the leaving.

The meeting continued well into the evening ending with everyone in agreement that the men who were called to service would escort the women and children of Gravesend to either New Amsterdam or Fort Amersfoort. The two groups would leave at 7:00 am.

Lady Moody said good-bye to the last person and closed the door behind her. There would be little time to pack anything, but the only thing she really cared about was Henry. The night was just about to get longer for her.

"Mother, I would like to talk with you" Henry began almost the instant she shut the door.

"Yes, dear, what is it?" Lady Moody was exhausted, but she always made time for Henry, especially on the rare occasion when he wanted to talk.

"Mother…" he began, pausing as if he was searching for the right words. "I want to join the men in their military service tomorrow."

Lady Moody's heart skipped a beat and her breath left her body. She sat down hard on the nearest chair. She did not want to over react, but there was no way she was going to let her sixteen year old son join the military, and especially not Kieft's military!

"Henry, I know you think you are a man now…" she began

He cut her off "I am a man, Mother."

"Yes, you are a man. But, Henry, you are a young man. You have a few more years before you have to make that decision."

"No, Mother. My time is now. I will go with the men tomorrow."

"Why, son? Why do you want to go tomorrow instead of waiting just a while longer?"

"Mother, I am sixteen. My father was not much older than I when he served. I helped in last week's raid and I have helped in the few times before that in the smaller fights. I am ready."

Lady Moody's eyes welled up, but she would not let him see her cry about this. She was strong and he needed a strong mother now. "Henry, I cannot let you do this. You are my son. I love you. I beg of you to take my advice and just wait a little longer before you enter

CHAPTER 10

into the military if that is what you want to do. All I am asking is for you to take some time to think about this."

"I have thought about it. My friends, the Indians, who are my age and even younger, are considered full grown. I am a man and I will go with the men tomorrow and pull my weight. It is my duty."

Lady Moody could see that there was no talking to him. He had made up his mind that he was going with or without her blessing. At this very moment he looked and acted so much like his father, so strong, so determined, and so stubborn. Simultaneously she loved Henry Sr. and hated him for giving her such a son. Henry had reached manhood and felt he had to prove himself in this world. She knew the time was coming, but she had hoped it would not be this soon and in this way.

After a long pause she spoke. "Very well, Henry. I cannot stop you."

Henry kissed his mother and tried to assure her that everything would be all right. She pretended not to worry and that she believed he was full grown. But, no matter what the age a son becomes, his mother always sees the baby she gave birth to, nursed from her breast, and taught all his life. She suddenly felt so old.

Penelope and Richard were in the kitchen and saw Henry go into his room. Although they did not want to overhear the mother-son private conversation, they could not help but hear. They went into the living room where Lady Moody was sitting, trying to hold in her grief.

"I will take the boy with me. Will and I will make sure he comes back to you safely" said Richard.

Lady Moody gave a half smile. She knew that if Henry was determined to go, then Richard and William were the two she wanted him to be with. "Thank you, sir. I know you will do your best to keep him safe."

"It would be ridiculous for me to say don't worry, but try not to. Just pray for us each day and that will help more than anything."

"Yes. I had already intended on doing that."

She was ready to change the subject so she looked at Penelope and got up. "Well, Baroness, we need to find you a place to stay."

"Yes, with all the excitement today I did not know how to ask about that" said Penelope.

"Lady Moody has agreed for you to stay with her. Is that acceptable to you?" asked Richard.

Penelope had liked what she saw in Lady Moody from the start, but felt admiration for her from the time she had heard her in Kieft's office. "Yes, I would like that very much."

"Then it is settled" said Lady Moody. "My dear, would you mind if we changed your dress?"

Penelope looked down at what she was wearing and smiled. "I guess I do look out of place here. I have no money to buy a dress. I have nothing but what I am wearing."

"Captain Jacobson has taken care of that" said Richard.

Penelope looked surprise. "What do you mean?"

"Captain Jacobson sent this money," said Lady Moody holding out the purse, "to take care of your needs. So, don't worry about a new dress or a place to stay. We will take care of you until we find out about your family. Besides, I have dresses here you can wear until we can make a few of your own. We can get a bolt of cloth in town."

"I don't know how to thank you both" said Penelope.

"You don't have to" said Richard.

Richard left and went to his house to inform his servants of what was going on. He was going to send them to New Amsterdam where he had some land holdings. They were to attend to his property and house there until he returned. He could trust George, Anna, and the others to be loyal. They were really more like part of his family than servants. Besides, George almost had his debt paid off and would soon start working on Anna's.

The next morning the two groups dispersed to the two forts. The men who left their families at Fort Amersfoort met up with the others the next day at New Amsterdam. No one had time to gather many belongings. They had to leave Gravesend quickly and move lightly. The original charter that Lady Moody held for Gravesend somehow got lost in all the confusion and Kieft had conveniently lost his copy.

CHAPTER 10

They would have to start all over again.

Director General Kieft had heard about the men of Gravesend and how well they had handled their Indian attack. So, he wanted them to guard New Amsterdam and him. The men did so, but with bad tastes in their mouths. Some of the men were allowed to go to Fort Amersfoort where they had their families, which was about the only decent thing Kieft did for them, and he only did it then because he was trying to get back in Lady Moody's good graces.

Lady Moody stayed at Fort Amersfoort for several months and then moved to New Amsterdam. Thomas Applegate had invited Penelope and her to stay with them for a while, hoping things would soon quiet. The Applegate's were good friends and good hosts to Lady Moody, but too talkative for Penelope's tastes. She had gotten used to the quieter, slower pace of the Indian village and missed that sense of easiness. Their talkative nature also got them into trouble at New Amsterdam where suing for slander was as common as getting a drink of water. Penelope, already self-conscious about her scars, did not need or want the added attention they brought to themselves.

The one thing she did like about the Applegate residence was that it was close to where Richard was stationed. He had gotten into the habit of stopping by Thomas' house once or twice a week to visit as time allowed. She grew to respect and admire him and even began to have deep feelings for him. He never showed pity for her, nor treated her in a demeaning manner for what she had been through. It was different from the feelings she had for Kent, but deeply ingrained all the same.

Lady Moody liked the residence because it was close to Henry. She didn't follow him around like a nosy mother, but she was at least able to see her son once in a while and it helped her feelings. Henry wouldn't admit it, but it helped his feelings, too. He was able to protect his mother when she was this close.

Penelope posted several letters over the next months to her father telling him what had happened in the time she had been gone. She did not get a reply for over a year. Finally, she received a letter from one of her father's parishners in Holland. Mr. Thomson came down with the fever just weeks after Penelope left for the Americas, the letter said. He never recovered and died soon afterwards. Penelope had no living family left. She was alone in the world.

Kieft's ineptness grew. The Indian skirmishes were getting more and more frequent. Last week Bowne and Stout had returned to Gravesend to see how things were. They found that it had been ransacked and the only building left standing was Lady Moody's house. The entire settlement would have to be rebuilt.

When she first arrived at New Amsterdam Lady Moody was despondent over the situation. She wondered if the best thing for her to do was to go back to the Bay Colony where she still owned property. She hated the thought of going back there, but she felt as if it might be safest. Had she done the right thing by starting Gravesend? She had believed in it so. She spent several afternoons with Penelope talking of these things. Penelope did not tell her what to do, instead she just listened as Mrs. Moody talked and figured things out for herself. It seemed to be the best medicine. Lady Deborah finally realized that she was not a quitter. She became resolute in her ambition. Gravesend would be settled, Indians or no.

Lady Moody then considered it her job to see that she had a new charter in her hand from the director general so that she could go back to her beloved Gravesend as soon as possible. She pestered him until he finally agreed and to her surprise, was able to get the charter drawn up much faster than the last one. Most of the original patentees wanted to participate in the second charter. However, some chose not to, some had gotten sick and died, and some moved elsewhere.

After two years, the Dutch began to suffer from war fatigue. Kieft was even beginning to get tired of it. He wanted one final annihilation of the aborigines and to make it decisive, cruel, and back-breaking.

He sent several thousand of his outlying troops to one of the Indian villages that had been at war with the Dutch. The men's orders were to execute every living native. The Dutch military fulfilled their duty, killing over 1600 men, women, and children in just one night. They did not leave even an insect moving and burned anything they

CHAPTER 10

didn't kill. The babies were found stabbed and run-through with swords while still attached to their backboards. Mothers were found over the bodies of their dead children having died trying protect them. The Indian men had been caught off guard, but had put up as much fight as they could, even though they were so outnumbered.

When the other villages found out about the devastating cruelty of the latest massacre they agreed to a truce. Beaten and defeated, the Indians signed a peace treaty with the lecherous Director Governor Kieft, ending the two year Indian war. There may have been a peace treaty, but trust was never there…on either side.

Finally, the Gravesend patentees would be able to return home. The men celebrated the end of the hated war by burning their uniforms. Baxter and Hubbard, especially, began to harbor an intense dislike of the Dutch. They began noticing how much English influence was growing and to think that perhaps the English would be better to cast their lots with than the Dutch.

The night of the peace treaty signing Richard came to Applegate's door. He was dressed in his finest to call on Baroness Van Princes. He sat on the porch with her for about an hour. It amazed Penelope that a man this brave could be this scared when it came to matters of the heart.

He was a simple man, but tonight he wanted to be fancy, elaborate. It was just not in him to have so many words. Finally he got his nerve. "Baroness," he began "we have known each other for almost two years. In that time I have come to love you as I have no other in my life. Would you do me the honor of marrying me?"

Penelope felt her heart leap from her chest. She felt such a strong feeling for him that she could not contain herself. "I would like nothing more than to be your wife."

They kissed. It was a fervent kiss not at all like anything Richard had ever known. He had kissed women before, but never one with this much passion. Penelope had lived so much life in her twenty-two years; she could not help but have more passion than any other woman. It was the best idea he ever had, he thought, getting this woman to marry him. He saw no scar, no handicap, nothing but her beauty and her loyalty.

The Applegate's and Lady Moody were thrilled with the news of the impending nuptials. This night was the best in a great while for Lady Moody. Henry had returned to her unharmed. William and Richard had kept him safe, just as they promised. Henry had proven himself to be a man and his mother was prouder of him than she ever thought she could be. They could finally go home in peace and start that life anew.

Chapter 11

Starting Over

The patentees of the second charter were able to have the signatures made official on December 19, 1645. This time there was no taking of one's word in the matter of negotiations. Everything was done in writing and every patentee received a copy signed by the director general. No one would be held hostage to a bureaucrat again.

William Kieft's last official act was to issue the second charter to Gravesend. After numerous complaints from people within his administration and years of corruption, he was finally recalled to Holland by the West India Company. He never made it back to receive his admonishment. The *Princess*, the ship in which Kieft and Parson Bogardus were traveling, wrecked off the coast of England. Nothing was ever found of the passengers or their cargo as everything was lost at sea. All the treasures that Kieft had built for himself perished at the bottom of the ocean in a form of poetic justice that so rarely happens.

The West India Company selected Peter Stuyvesant to be the new director general. He was a testy, irritable man with a right wooden leg studded with silver nails and a nasty reputation for getting his own way. He had two nicknames, "Peg Leg Pete" and "Old Silver Nails." Many attributed his foul nature to his prosthesis that did not fit very well and he used often to call meetings to order or to protest something someone said. He had little tolerance for those outside the Dutch Reform Church faith, but since the Gravesend charter had already established freedom of religion, there was little he could do about it there.

However, Lady Moody soon melted the man in her usual charming way and it wasn't long before he was visiting her home in Gravesend to speak with her, asking for her opinion on government matters and borrow a book or two from her impressive library. Once again, Lady Moody had charmed a director general. This one, however, she genuinely liked and regarded.

Starting over would not be easy, but "nothing worth doing is ever easy" was Lady Moody's motto. She had convinced Penelope and Richard to take their wedding vows in the church that was being rebuilt in Gravesend. The men were almost finished with the exterior construction, liking only a roof. She had insisted that the reception be held at her house with a celebratory atmosphere. It had been so long since the settlers had something to celebrate so this was to be an extra joyous occasion for everyone. Lady Moody even hired a few musicians to make the evening even more festive.

New houses were going up all over. Richard was intent on finishing his house as soon as he could. He wanted a new house and a new bride and lots of children to fill it. Every day he waited for Penelope seemed longer and longer. After all, he wasn't getting any younger. He was already forty two and she twenty two.

Richard ordered a very special bolt of silk for Penelope's wedding dress, even though she had protested saying she did not want anything that fancy. The one thing she did want was for Owehela and especially Nalehileehque to attend her wedding ceremony. Richard made sure that her surrogate family knew of the upcoming event.

The day of the wedding finally arrived in the spring of 1646. Richard chose William Bowne to serve as best man and Penelope

CHAPTER 11

chose Lady Moody as matron of honor. Penelope insisted that Owehela walk her down the aisle. While there was some concern over what others would think, Richard finally said that others' opinions should not be a factor. Penelope could have whomever she wanted in her wedding. Obadiah Holmes was the preacher conducting the ceremony. Everyone in Gravesend attended the late afternoon wedding held under the newly rebuilt church roof. Afterwards, the whole settlement joined the bride and groom at Lady Moody's house for the much anticipated party.

The musicians that Lady Moody had hired for the festivities were more than Penelope had hoped for. They played lively music to which many of the settlers danced jigs. She felt a little guilty for all the gayety for in the back of her mind she could just hear how her father would have a fit if he knew she had danced. But she wanted to dance and to sing and to enjoy this precious life that was almost taken so early.

She looked at her new husband as he was laughing with the other men and wondered at the beauty that was he. Never had she known such a man. He came searching for her even though all looked lost. He helped his friends, even at his own expense at times. He loved life and freedom...and her.

How can this man love me? she thought. *I am so horribly scarred and what if I cannot have children?*

The abdominal scar was prominent, but no one had seen it since she had been with the whites. He did not know the severity of it and she had never really discussed it with him. There was no hiding it tonight. At least when she had been with Kent she had been beautiful and unscarred. Now look at her. Would he even find her attractive? How much of a wife could she be to him without children? How she prayed for children!

When the evening was winding down Richard found his bride who had been speaking with Nalehileehque for quite a while. "It's time we went home" whispered Richard in her ear.

Shyly she smiled and got up and announced that she was tossing the bouquet. She went to the porch as all the single ladies waited below. With one toss of her right hand the bouquet was in the air and soon landing in the hands of Lydia Holmes, Obadiah's daughter. Lydia glanced at William's sixteen year old son John and smiled as he blushed. Everyone laughed at the awkward teens while Richard and Penelope ran through the crowd to the carriage that waited. George was driving them just around the corner to their house. It was not far at all, but Richard did not want Penelope to get her new silk dress dirty. Neither did she, for she had hope against hope that she could one day have a daughter in order that she may pass the dress on.

Richard and Penelope exited the carriage and George went to the barn to put the horse up for the night. Like any new husband, Richard picked up his new bride and carried her across the threshold. He put her down with a kiss.

She knew she had to tell him now, before they went any farther. "Richard, I have something to tell you."

"Shhhhh. Don't say anything." He just kept on kissing her neck.

"No, Richard. I have to tell you now. You may not want me after I tell you this."

Looking at her with a smile he said "there is nothing you can tell me that will make me not want you. You are my wife. I love you. That is all I need to know."

She looked at him for a second and thought how she loved him so. "Richard, I was not just scalped and my arm crippled." She stopped and turned away from him for she could not look at him while she spoke this. She had to blurt it out or she would loose her nerve. "I was also severely wounded in my abdomen during the attack on the beach. It was so bad that my intestines shown through. I do not know if I can have children or not. Nalehileehque did all she could do to help me, but I just don't know."

Richard turned her around to face him. He brushed back a small tuft of hair that stuck out past her ornate headpiece that she had made to wear instead of a veil. "Penelope, I married you for who you are, not what you can give me. Yes, I want children and I hope God blesses us with many, but my deepest desire is you. You are the woman I want."

CHAPTER 11

"Why? You saw the scar left on my head from the scalping when you came to get me, why would you want a woman with only one good arm and scars so hideous?"

Again Richard smiled at her "because those scars are part of who you are and I love all of who you are. I have never known anyone like you. I knew that I was going to marry you the instant I laid eyes on you, even when you were beating poor old Danel."

She smiled. "I was pretty mean to him, wasn't I?"

He smiled back "he could take it."

With that she flung her arms around his neck and kissed him with a passion that neither knew they held. He picked her up and carried her into the bedroom where all the desires of the past few years and the emotions of the time were released in all their splendor.

Penelope had learned more than just how to make pottery and grow a good garden from the Indians. They were uninhibited people with not much privacy in the huts. Penelope had seen and heard the unbridled sensuality that they enjoyed in their lovemaking. It was so different from the night she and Kent had made love which was so awkward. She was anxious to finally participate in a way that she had witnessed and Richard was just as willing to enjoy the fruits of her learning. She just asked that they keep the lamp turned off so that she would not be so self-conscious in her appearance. Richard didn't care about the way she looked, but was willing to respect her wishes.

A few months later, Penelope began to get sick, especially when she cooked. Anna helped all she could, but nothing seemed to help the sickness. Lady Moody came to visit and noticed how pale Penelope was. When asked about how she was feeling, Penelope replied that she was having trouble keeping food down.

Lady Moody smiled. "I suspect, my dear, that you are with child."

Penelope laughed. "No. I don't think so. I just have trouble keeping things down."

Lady Moody looked at the young bride with a knowing grin. "When was your last menstrual cycle?"

Penelope knew that Lady Deborah could be blunt, but this was almost rude, but she felt compelled to answer the question. "Not since before Richard and I were married."

Lady Moody raised her eyebrows and tilted her head. Saying those words out loud made Penelope's thoughts become reality. Could she really be with child? Could God be so good to her this way? She had to find out for sure. She had to see Nalehileehque.

She hugged Lady Deborah and got up fast. She ran out to see Richard. He had to take her across the bay to see Nalehileehque today. She found him in the field tending to a newborn calf.

"Richard, please take me to see Nalehileehque. I have to see her today."

"What is the hurry?"

"Please, Richard. Please don't ask any questions. I will tell you everything after I see Nalehileehque."

Penelope asked for so little, he felt that this must be important to her or she would not have asked today. He finished cleaning the calf and making sure the cow would accept it. Then, he loaded Penelope in their little boat and sailed across the bay to the village where he had found Penelope those years ago. It would be the first time Penelope had been back since she had left with him.

They made it to the village and Penelope went immediately to Owehela's hut. She spoke to Nalehileehque in their language, the one that Richard could not understand. Richard waited outside while the women talked, not really knowing what was going on. Penelope had brought a bushel of strawberries as a gift for her adopted mother and that was all he knew about this trip.

After about an hour Penelope emerged from the hut with Nalehileehque and a smile. She told Richard that Owehela and Tateuscung were off hunting and were not there today and that they could go back home now. By this time it was getting dark so Nalehileehque insisted they stay till morning. Richard was still confused.

Penelope took Richard by the hand and put it on her scarred abdomen. "Sir, we are with child" she said.

Richard lost his breath. He wanted to laugh and cry and shout, but could not get the air into his lungs to do those things. So, he just

CHAPTER 11

picked up his wife and swung her around in the gentlest way he knew how.

"Is everything all right" he asked when he finally could speak.

"Nalehileehque said that everything looks fine and that we should be able to have healthy children" replied Penelope.

That evening Nalehileehque gave Penelope some medicine for her sickness. It should go away soon, but in the mean time the herbs would help. Richard assured his adopted mother-in-law that he would make sure that Penelope was taken care of. Seeing how he treated her, Nalehileehque was not worried.

The next morning they sailed back across the bay to their home at Gravesend. Penelope confirmed her pregnancy to Lady Moody who was ecstatic. The baby would be here in about six months and there was much to do.

The months passed quickly and it was soon time for the baby to come. Richard sailed across the bay, sometimes having to cut through the ice, to get Nalehileehque for that is who Penelope wanted to do the midwife duties. He got her to his home just in time because the labor pains had started just that morning. By the time Nalehileehque got to her, the pains were only three minutes apart. The labor was excruciating for Penelope and the waiting was difficult for Richard.

In the kitchen Richard could hear the songs that Nalehileehque sang to Penelope during her labor. That voice was so soothing that it even helped calm his nerves. He could understand why Penelope depended on her so much. Anna cooked and made pots of coffee for him while he waited, but he could neither eat nor drink.

Lady Moody came that evening to check on the progress. She was hoping that there would be a new baby to see, but the labor had not gone as fast as hoped. She tried to pass the time with Richard who was distracted and paced the floor. He tried going outside for a smoke on his pipe, but even that didn't calm him.

Finally, at about ten o'clock that evening a loud wail filled the air inside and outside the house. John Stout announced his arrival with a vengeance. Everyone stopped when the cry was heard, smiled, and sighed a sigh of relief before congratulating each other as if they had done something spectacular instead of Penelope.

Nalehileehque came out of the bedroom holding a small bundle that wiggled and cried. She smiled and nodded to Richard. Immediately he came over to her and took the little bundle in his arms. It was such a contrast of sizes to see this large man with huge hands holding such a tiny bundle so delicately.

He took the baby back to his mother in the bed. Penelope smiled at her husband and he kissed her forehead. "You have given me the greatest gift" he said holding back his tears. "I love you more than I can say."

"I love you, too" said Penelope.

So was the birth of the first of their ten children, seven boys and three girls. Each time Nalehileehque was there to deliver her child. Penelope and Richard would have it no other way.

Chapter 12

Epilogue

Baptist Town, New Jersey

Penelope and Richard lived at Gravesend for four years and in those years had three children, all boys. Life was good at first in Gravesend. That is, until everyone began to get sue-happy. The settlers began to sue each other for slander over the smallest and silliest things.

For instance Nicholas Stillwell on one occasion accused Thomas Applegate of slander for Thomas allegedly saying that Stillwell did not have enough money to pay off all his debts. Hubbard and Baxter, and even Baxter's son Thomas sued Applegate at every turn for any little remark they considered to be offensive. Often one would sue and the others would sit on the jury, making it very difficult for poor Thomas to get a fair trial. Yes, he did speak too much but he rarely, if ever, got a fair shake at trial either. Applegate was an easy target and they held target practice often.

After four years the pressure was getting to be too much for Richard and for Penelope especially. Somehow she had even gotten mixed up in the slander suits when she was visiting Eliza Applegate. She was accused of saying that Mrs. Ambrose had milked Eliza's cow. She had never said such a thing, but seeing that no one would listen to reason she finally apologized for the whole episode and everyone was satisfied. But it took a trial and an apology, which she did not owe, to put the whole thing to rest.

After this, she wanted to leave Gravesend and move closer to Nalehileehque and Owehela. They were getting older and she longed to be near them. Richard was inclined to agree since the atmosphere had gotten so hostile in the new settlement and he was always ready to start something new. The togetherness they once had felt toward their neighbors was being offset by the rush to trial over silly things.

It did not help matters that Hubbard and Baxter were making noises about aliening with the English instead of the Dutch. The relationship between the Dutch and the English was intensifying so it would only be a matter of time before some would want to turn Gravesend into an English controlled town instead of a Dutch controlled one. All it would take was a little interest on the part of the English and Gravesend would be theirs.

Richard and Penelope decided to go speak with Owehela. They wanted to find out if there was a way they could buy some land in that area. They sailed across the bay to the Indian village.

"Hë" said Richard (which means "hello" in English) to Owehela upon arriving at his home.

"Hello" replied Owehela. He loved to practice his English whenever he got the opportunity.

"It is good to see you my friend" said Richard.

"And to see you" was the reply.

Penelope went into the hut straightway to see Nalehileehque. She had brought strawberries and peaches as gifts. They sat down to talk for a while and catch up on the events since they last spoke. Nalehileehque told Penelope that Tateuscung's new wife was expecting a child soon and that had made the whole family happy.

Outside, the two men were already talking about land. Richard explained that he and Penelope wanted to move closer to their village

CHAPTER 12

and asked if he could purchase some land for their home.

"Only Popomora can decide that. He lives near here. We will go see him and you can ask him if he will sell you land" explained Owehela.

"Thank you" said Richard.

Richard and Penelope stayed there for the night. George and Anna were taking care of the children so they did not worry about hurrying back to their home. Penelope enjoyed her time with Nalehileehque and helping her prepare their supper. Richard seemed right at home with Owehela and it was apparent that they enjoyed getting to know each other.

The next morning Richard and Owehela went to Popomora's village to speak to him about a land purchase. The old sachem welcomed them to his home. Richard spoke in the Lenape language which impressed Popomora greatly. He considered it a sign of respect for the white man to speak Lenape instead of demanding English be spoken. Penelope had taught Richard as much of the language as she knew so he was able to be comfortable speaking it.

Richard explained that he and his family wanted to live on this side of the bay in peace beside the Indians. They were not looking to fight or take over. They just wanted to start a settlement and be good neighbors.

Popomora asked how many whites would want to live there. He was concerned about his people being pushed out. Richard said that only a few at first, but possibly as many as 200. (There were already over 500 Indians nearby.) They were peaceful people and did not want war. Owehela vouched for Stout, and Owehela's word went a long way with Popomora.

At the end of the talks it was agreed that Richard would go back to Gravesend and find out exactly how many families would like to come with them. Then, Popomora would talk trade for the land. Richard vowed to come back in one week with more information.

Richard and Penelope returned to their home at Gravesend with renewed hope. Richard was ready for another adventure. Penelope was ready for a new start with her young family and her adopted parents. She dearly loved Lady Moody and her sons loved her as a grandmother, but the pull to come across the bay was getting stronger. Lady Moody would never move. She had grown to cherish her life at Gravesend.

Richard gathered a few of his friends together at his house. Obadiah Holmes and his son Jonathan, James Ashton, William Bowne and his son John, Samuel Spicer, and James Grover came to hear what Richard had to say about this land across the bay. Although Jonathan Holmes and John Bowne were young, their fathers wanted them to start acquiring land in their own rights as soon as they could.

Richard explained about the good land across the bay and how the Indians were friendly. They could start a settlement over there away from the legal entanglements that were beginning to fester in this atmosphere. The men that were gathered at Richard's kitchen table leaned toward the Baptist religious beliefs which would make the settlers have even more in common. There was much to be done. The land at Gravesend did not need much clearing when they arrived as the Indians had done most of it before they purchased it. But across the bay, trees needed to be felled and overgrowth cut so the land could be cleared for plowing.

Each man listened about the proposition that Stout offered. They remembered how Gravesend had to be settled twice and how Kieft had betrayed them. Did they really want to start all over? They told a hopeful Stout that they would go home and think it over and give him an answer tomorrow evening at about this same time.

The next evening every man that had been at the table the evening before was interested in the settlement. However, they wanted to go look at the land first. That was understandable to Richard so he agreed to take the men across the bay in his boat the next morning.

By nine o'clock the next morning they were touring the property. It was good land that could produce a profitable income for the farms planned there. Popomora met the men who were with Richard and was impressed with their peaceful demeanor and they with his. He agreed to sell them the land.

The men were very excited with what they saw and sailed back

CHAPTER 12

across the bay with each man agreeing to join in this new prospect. They brought the tribute that Popomora asked, made a peace treaty, and the deal was done. They agreed to name their new town Baptist Town.

The families stayed at Gravesend while the men worked on clearing the land for the crops. Some, like William Bowne, never moved there, but owned property. His son, John, grew in stature and in his later years was a wonderful statesman for Baptist Town, later called Middletown.

They had purchased the land from the Indians, but they still had to make the deal with the government at New Amsterdam for legal settlement rights. Many times over the years the men spoke with director general Peter Stuyvesant about securing rights. The original five families had now turned into twelve seeking a patent from the director general.

Finally, in 1660, twelve years after the first five families sought out the land across the bay, they received their patent from Stuyvesant. James Grover had surveyed the property and gotten the papers for the necessary paperwork. The land was divided into lots. Richard drew lot number 6.

They worked for several years after their first arrival in 1648 building houses and barns and preparing for the families. John Bowne was growing into manhood and worked especially hard helping Richard make things ready. He was determined to be a well propertied member of the community.

The Stouts moved their family to the new settlement as soon as Richard had his house built. Penelope was happy being so close to her adopted family. They visited each other often and her children thought of Owehela and Nalehileehque as their grandparents. They kept their Gravesend property and even increased it by buying land that came up for sale close to their patent. Richard, in effect, managed to work two settlements.

Young John Bowne had the gift of standing up for his convictions. He was not haughty or boastful or even very talkative. He was steady, logical, humble, and well educated. After working alongside him in the clearing of the land, Richard knew that he would be an asset to the community. As his own son John Stout grew older, Richard took him with them to work on the new property.

Not long after Penelope, who was pregnant with her fourth child, brought her young family to the new farm Owehela came to see her. She invited him in to lunch with her family, but he would not enter her house. She knew something was wrong.

"Tell me what is wrong" said Penelope to the old man.

"I have heard some disturbing news" said Owehela. "I have brought a canoe for you to take your family away from this area."

"Why?" asked Penelope. "Why do you want me to take my family away?"

Owehela was obviously disturbed by the news he had to bring. "I have heard some of the talk by other tribes. They are planning to attack your homes and destroy all the whites."

Penelope went pale. "How can they do this? We have purchased the land and paid the price that Popomora asked. Why do they want to attack us?"

"They are not our people. These are others. They think you are here to hurt them."

"I must find Richard immediately" said Penelope.

She ran across the field to the back side of the farm, Owehela right behind her. Richard was plowing some new ground with a team of mules. He looked up and stopped what he was doing when he saw Penelope and Owehela running toward him.

"What's wrong?" he asked.

"Owehela said that our homes are going to be attacked tonight. We must leave" Penelope said out of breath.

He looked toward the old Indian. "Where did you hear this?"

Owehela did not want to explain where he had heard this information. He could already be killed if any who planned tonight's raid found out he had told the whites. "It does not matter where I heard it. They are going to burn your homes tonight. Your family must leave."

Richard was doubtful. There had been no problems with the

CHAPTER 12

Indians since they had been there. Surely the old man misunderstood. "Maybe it was just talk. We haven't had any trouble since we have been here. And if it is true, they were probably talking about somewhere else."

Penelope's anger burned. How could Richard be so nonchalant? The fire that burned in her all those years before when she had to stand up to the authoritarians in her life erupted like a volcano.

"Richard! Owehela has never told me anything to make me doubt him. I am taking the children and we are going to New Amsterdam. I would like it if you came with us, but we are going all the same."

With that she and Owehela went back to her house and collected her children. They went to the water where he had left a dugout canoe so that she could transport her family. She put her three boys into the canoe and paddled as best she could with her good arm towards New Amsterdam.

Still in the field, Richard began to think about what had just happened. Penelope was convinced that there would be a raid tonight and Owehela had never lied to them. Could she be right? He thought for a moment and decided that it would be better to be safe. He brought his team of mules to the barn and unharnessed them.

He went to the surrounding houses and told them what Penelope and Owehela had told him. The men decided to do as they did back in Gravesend. They would wait on the Indians to attack and repel them if they came. The other men were more easily convinced of the information than Richard had been.

That night at about midnight, just as Owehela had said, a band of Indians began to attack. Forty men gathered at Richard's house waiting on the ambush. The men fired their guns at the advancing raiders who only carried primitive weapons and killed several. Seeing that they were not surprising the whites the Indians retreated to regroup.

During the lull, Richard advanced. He called to the leader of the raid saying "ktälenixsi hach?" which means in Lenape, "Do you speak Lenape?"

They were not Lenape, but seeing that this white man knew a

form of their language the leader agreed to a meeting that night.

Richard, James Grover, and young John Bowne met the three leaders of the raid half way between their two forces. Richard spoke in Lenape, which was close enough in dialect that the leaders could understand him. He explained that the whites had guns and the Indians did not. They wanted peace, not trouble, but if trouble was what they wanted they could get it. He was firm in making the leader, known as Tamenend, understand that he did not want to fight, but would and fight hard, if need be.

Tamenend needed to save face, but did not come directly out to say that. He knew that fighting more would mean loosing more of his men and he could ill afford it. He also realized after speaking with the three delegates that these men were not the type of whites they had encountered before. Stout, Grover, and Bowne, for their part, understood Tamenend's predicament.

The three white men needed to speak amongst themselves for a few minutes. After excusing themselves for the few minutes they returned with a proposition for Tamenend. They offered him 3 hogsheads of tobacco, 3 horses, one of each from Stout, Grover, and Bowne, and some wampum as a sign of goodwill if he would make a peace treaty with them.

Smiling Tamenend agreed. Everyone was the winner. Tamenend was able to save face with his people by receiving gifts or tribute and Baptist Town was offered a peaceful existence. They agreed to a celebration the next day for the signing of the treaty.

Richard went and found his family and Owehela. He apologized to his old friend for doubting him. Then he told Penelope of what had happened and about the agreement. They returned home and celebrated with all the settlers and their new friends, the Indians, over the peace treaty that was signed that day. It was a good agreement in which everyone on both sides held his word. When surrounding settlements were having problems with raids and attacks, Baptist Town was able to keep peace because of their keeping of their word and the treaty.

Even though they managed to keep the peace with the Indians, the

CHAPTER 12

time became again tumultuous for the settlers. In 1664 the English sailed into the harbor at New Amsterdam, and although the fort was defended by 20 cannons, the people, being tired of the Dutch administration, refused to resist the English invaders. Stuyvesant was forced to surrender to the English and returned to Holland in disgrace to the West India Company who blamed him for everything that went wrong. He eventually sailed back to America and lived out the remainder of his life on a farm in New Amsterdam.

The patent that had been granted by the Dutch for Baptist Town, now known as Middletown was voided by the English. Their king, Charles II, granted the northeastern coast to his brother, James the Duke of York, and installed a new governor Richard Nichols. The patentees would now have to negotiate with the English for the land they had settled for several years all over again.

Richard Nichols, however, agreed to grant the patent for which the twelve asked on April 8, 1665. The grant required that they grow the settlement to at least one hundred families within three years of the date of the patent. They were given the same freedoms that the Dutch had agreed to including freedom of religion, the right to build villages at places of their own selection, and authority to erect courts for the trial for small causes. They could even elect representatives with full power to make their own laws and constitutions.

The English divided the territory up into colonies and called them New York and New Jersey. New Amsterdam's name was changed to New York as well. The English brought with them a better order of bookkeeping than the Dutch used. It was not perfect, but more in order.

Most of the people became known as Baptist, as the name implied. The first Baptist church for the state of New Jersey eventually started in Middletown, meeting first in people's homes and then in a church that was later built. Penelope, Richard, and their children became charter members of the church that became known as Hopewell Baptist. John Bowne, one of Middletown's most prominent leaders, became a Quaker. All lived in peace with each other and their neighbors.

AS GOOD AS DEAD

Richard lived to reach almost 90 years of age. Penelope went on to live to the ripe old age of 110, living long enough to see her offspring grow to number over 500. Although they did not live to see it, the Stout family settled land all down the east coast on to the south, starting Baptist churches wherever they went.

The Benedict's History of the Baptists, which was published in 1790 recorded the Stout family this way: "The origin of this Baptist family is no less remarkable: for they all sprang from one woman, and she as good as dead; her history is in the mouths of most of her posterity…"